"Legacy's Dawn"

M/M Wolf Shifter Paranormal Romance

Secrets of Lycanthia Volume 3

Apollo Surge

This book is intended for Adults (ages 18+) only. The contents may be offensive to some readers. It may contain graphic language, explicit sexual content, and adult situations. May contain scenes of unprotected sex. Please do not read this book if you are offended by content as mentioned above or if you are under the age of 18. Please educate yourself on safe sex practices before making potentially life-changing decisions about sex in real life.

This story is a work of fiction. Names, characters, businesses, places, events and incidents are the products of the author's imagination or used in a fictitious manner and are not to be construed as real. Any resemblance to actual persons, living or dead, or actual events is purely coincidental. Products or brand names mentioned are trademarks of their respective holders or companies. The cover uses licensed images and are shown for illustrative purposes only. Any person(s) that may be depicted on the cover are simply models.

Edition v1.00 (2021.02.08)
apollo@apollosurge.com

Special thanks to the following volunteer readers who helped with proofreading: RB, Blue Savannah, Rudy and those who assisted but wished to be anonymous. Thank you so much for your support.

Prologue

King Stewart sat on his cold throne, narrowed eyes staring at his great prize. A thin smile played upon his grey lips, and the dim light that penetrated the narrowed windows of his castle cast his face in a grim pallor. The plan had worked perfectly. The wolves had taken his bait, just as he knew they would. Now Casper was by his side again and everything was right with the world. The kingdom of Silvain would rise again and take its place after everything that had been taken from it by those damned monsters in Lycanthia.

He had something precious in his possession now; the king of Lycanthia. Boris von Arnheim himself. Stewart clasped his hands and he was unable to stop a dry, cracked laugh from emerging from his lips. Revenge had been on his mind for so long and the seeds of this plan had been planted for such a long time, it had been an ordeal to see them come to fruition. The tension had been almost unbearable, but now he could revel in his triumph, although there was still much to be done.

"Look at him father, he's pathetic," Casper spat. The young prince had done well at hiding his disdain for the wolves during his time in Lycanthia, even pretending that he could ever fall in love with the wolf princess. Casper walked towards the captured king, who was on his knees, with silver shackles around his wrists and ankles, hurting him as well as keeping him captive. When Casper got too close Boris growled and lunged for him, only to collapse to the stone floor, clattering his jaw as he couldn't bring his hands to his defense. His face was already bruised, and the ugly welts were only getting worse. Casper scuttled back as Boris lunged, and Stewart laughed at his son's fear.

"Not so pathetic after all," he said. Casper glowered and gazed at Boris with revulsion in his eyes.

"What do you want from all this? What is your endgame?" Boris said. Every word had to be forced from his throat in a great effort, and blood trickled down his bruised lips.

"Your destruction," Stewart said. "Your downfall has been years in the making, generations in fact. My ancestors began planning our revenge as soon as your kind took what was rightfully ours."

"We took nothing of yours," the wolf king said.

"Are you really so deluded to believe that is true? You took everything. You took Lycanthia!" Stewart's fist came crashing down on the arm of his throne. The sound of the impact reverberated through the empty chamber.

Boris stared at him incredulously.

"Lycanthia was never yours. It was virgin land before we settled it."

"*We* had the rightful claim." Stewart's fist was still clenched. "Do you really believe that we wanted to stay here, in this cold and unforgiving land?" The king of Silvain gestured around the throne room. "Silvain has long been stripped of anything useful. Its resources have been depleted and it offers nothing but jagged stone and an icy heart. But Lycanthia…Lycanthia is filled with possibilities. It is where my family should have had its seat, but no, the wolves crawled in and decided to take it for themselves, ignoring our rightful claim. Well, the time has come for me to take it back. I shall take vengeance for all the wrongs done to this kingdom."

Boris snarled. "Do you really think you're going to take Lycanthia? If you think you're going to ransom me for a whole kingdom then you're even more of a fool than I thought you were. I'd rather die than allow you to march into Lycanthia and take it for yourself. What happened is in the past. It can't be changed now."

"Oh, you'll get your chance to die soon enough Boris," Stewart said with a cruel look in his beady eyes. "But here in Silvain we do not forget the transgressions of the past. And I'm not interested in taking Lycanthia. No, I have far greater plans than that. I'm going to rid the earth of you cursed wolves, and your blood is going to help me do it," he said.

"Let's kill him father. Let's slit his throat," hatred dripped off Casper's words. The boy was in a frenzy with vengeance and revenge. His hands were clenched into tight fists by his side and his entire body trembled. His voice was a shriek, so fueled with rage was he.

"No my son, not yet. He still has his uses for us," Stewart said, relaxing in the throne. He listened to the wolf king's protests, to the declarations of defiance and the promises that he was going to be stopped, but they were mere jokes to the Silvainian king. He knew that nothing could stop him. He had already won, and it was only a matter of time before his revenge was exacted fully.

He sat back in his throne and looked at the black abyss surrounding him. For so long now Silvain had been a place where hatred had festered. There had been little in the way of prosperity, and hope had been a forgotten virtue. The very air was laced with a fervent revenge, and now it was finally being fulfilled. The promises to his ancestors were being kept, and soon enough the wronged people of Silvain would have their revenge against the cursed and corrupt wolves, the abominations of nature. That fertile and beautiful land of Lycanthia had already been plunged into disarray with the loss of its king and the poisoning of their wolf princess, but more was to come, yes, much more. Stewart's heart thumped in his chest as he thought about his triumph. It was so near he could almost grasp it. Silvain would soon thrive again once the wolves were done away with. When the world was cleansed, he could take what was rightfully his, and there would be nobody to stop him.

Chapter One

The battle was still strong in Gregory's mind. Seeing the king being taken away and all the Lycanthian forces decimated by the enemy was a sight that would live long in his mind. The fear and terror had been etched into his heart and even now when he closed his eyes he trembled with dread, afraid that he was going to be caught. He hated leaving the King there, even though the king had ordered it, but there had been no other way. Not even the good news could temper the ill feeling in the pit of his heart; the news that he was going to be a father. In amongst everything that happened he had barely had a chance to process the news. A child, all of his own, with Jack. It was daunting and exciting in equal measure, but what kind of a world was he bringing his child into? A world of war? Of Chaos?

Emotions weighed heavily upon him as he sat by Leah's side. The princess had awoken from her slumber. The wound on her shoulder had lost its festering energy and she was no longer at the mercy of the poison that ran within her blood. She was awake, although she was still tired. Tristan and Shane had welcomed her back with hugs and everyone had rejoiced, but still nobody had told her all that had happened. Her weak hand rested in his. The bond of friendship was something she relied on now. Jack, Hank, Emily, and Shane had left the room to give Leah some peace. Her breathing was labored and it would take some time before she regained her strength.

"Father, Gregory, what has happened to me?" she said. Her hair fell upon her pale skin like strands of gold. Her lips were so pale they were translucent. Gregory's heart broke for her and he couldn't bear to bring himself to tell her what had happened. He glanced towards Tristan, who was trying to hold himself together after learning what had happened to the king. He walked up to the bed upon which his daughter laid and pressed his hand upon her forehead.

"I'm not sure where to start," he said, his voice trembling with emotion.

"What's happened? How long have I been asleep? What did…what did Casper do to me?" Leah asked. Anger flashed in her voice as she mentioned Casper's name. She visibly winced and Gregory assumed she was remembering the moment when he had hurled the spear at her.

"The spear he threw was laced with poison, a deadly poison for which there is no antidote. But we were told there was one. Boris led a force to meet with the King of Silvain where he was willing to make a trade for the cure, but it was all a trick. There was no cure. Gregory was there. He was the only one to return." Tristan's words choked on a sob.

"What do you mean he was the only one to return? What about father?" Leah's eyes went wide with panic. Gregory felt her hand tense against his. Her eyes fell upon him and demanded the truth. She tried to push herself up, but lacked the strength to do so.

"He's dead Leah. I'm sorry," Gregory said.

"No," Leah groaned. Then she repeated the word in a more defiant manner. "No, it can't be true. He can't die. Not like this. Tell me what happened at the battle. Why would they want him dead? Why would they do this?" she looked at Gregory directly.

"They hold some enmity towards Lycanthia because they feel they deserve this land. The King thinks we stole this place from his ancestors, and now he wants revenge. Boris wanted me to come back and tell of their treachery so that we could begin to plan for war."

"But what of father?"

"I'm sorry Leah. I tried to save him, but it was impossible. Your father commanded me to return. He's dead. He was being swarmed by a group of Silvainian soldiers. There's no way he could have survived. I'm sorry."

Leah's face dropped and it turned a whiter shade of pale, so much so that she looked like a ghost. Her hand fell from his and although he tried to grasp it, it slipped away from him. Guilt made his heart heavy. He wondered if he could have done more, or if he should have done more. Why had he been the only one to survive when so many others had died?

"I will make them pay for this," she said, summoning all her strength to turn her hands into balls. Her toes curled and her face turned into a snarl, before she lost the strength to hold her mood. She gasped and whimpered, annoyed that she was so weak.

"What is wrong with me..." she whispered. "This poison; you said there is no cure. Am I...am I dying too? I know that I feel different."

Gregory and Tristan glanced uneasily at each other. Gregory had no idea how Tristan was coping with this. Not only did he have to deal with the death of his husband, but he also had to tell his daughter that she had lost the ability to become a wolf. It was a most primal thing that had been ripped from her, and Gregory wondered if it had been worth it to give her half a life. People who weren't wolves wouldn't be able to understand the sacrifice or the scope of what she had lost. But Tristan would. He had been in love with a wolf, given birth to a wolf. More than anyone he would know the ramifications of the decision they had made.

"Leah," Tristan said, placing a hand upon her shoulder. "I know this is going to be difficult for you to hear. I want you to know that this was the only way to keep you from dying, and it was a decision made from love. When we found out there was no cure for the poison, we also found out it was directly attacking the wolf part of you. There is a relic called the Chalice of Sinterbaum. It was what helped give you life in the first place, and now it saved you again. It had the ability to give, and to take away…we…we decided that the only way to help you was to take away the part of you that the poison was attacking. We hoped that if it didn't have that to attack then it would lose its potency. We were right, but it came at a great cost. I'm afraid that you can no longer become a wolf."

The words fell through the air like a spear and stabbed Leah in the heart. Gregory could see her wince. Her brow crinkled and her lips trembled.

"No…it…it cannot be true. It is only temporary, surely. There must be some way to bring that part of me back," the words rushed out of her in a desperate tone.

Tristan shook his head solemnly. "There is no reversal. Even if there was, the poison would still be in your system and would start to attack you. This is the only way we could save your life. I know it's going to be difficult to cope, but I couldn't lose you Leah,"

Tristan clasped her hand and pressed his lips to her skin. Tears flowed down his cheeks. "Especially not now that your father has been taken from us." His head dropped and his body shuddered. Leah stared up at the ceiling.

"I feel as though I have awoken into a nightmare," she said, and swallowed a lump in her throat. "I am searching for something, something that is not there any longer. I feel so alone."

"You're not alone," Gregory said. "You still have me, and your family. You are still the princess, Leah. The kingdom needs you, as much as you need the kingdom."

"But how can I rule when I am only half of myself? What kind of queen would I be?" she asked in a mournful voice. Neither Gregory nor Tristan had an answer for her. Gregory had been thinking about sharing his good news with her, but it seemed like an inopportune time considering she was dealing with so much sorrow. Tristan looked up at Gregory.

"Would you mind giving Leah and I some time alone?" he asked. Gregory nodded and left her side, squeezing her hand before he left. He hoped she knew how much she was cared for, and that even though she had lost some precious part of herself it didn't mean that she was worthless. There was still a lot of life to live, even though it was a long road back from grief.

***

Gregory left the small chamber to where everyone else was waiting. Jack immediately came up to his side, noticing that he was suffering. Jack placed his arm on Gregory's shoulder, offering him some comfort.

"How did she take it?" Shane asked. Leah's grandfather's face was lined with worry.

"Not well," Gregory said, shrugging. "Tristan is talking with her now. It's a lot to take in."

"Yes, it is. I'm sure she will be well in time, but she will need you by her side, offering her comfort and support. These are going to be troubling times for everyone in Lycanthia. All that we thought was certain has been thrown into doubt," Shane said ominously. At this, Gregory noticed how Hank and Emily shared a worried look. They sidled closer to each other and their hands found each other.

"I'll be a friend to her. I just wish that I could have done more. If I had tried, perhaps I could have saved the King," Gregory said. Shane smiled reassuringly at him.

"You did all that you could have. By surviving you have given us a chance. We shall not be taken unawares by the enemy. But we must make preparations. Even though these are sad times there are duties that we must fulfill. I believe it is clear now that the kingdom of Silvain was working alone in this. We should free the prisoners," Shane said. "Would you see to this Gregory?"

"M-me?!" Gregory stammered. Shane smiled.

"You have been by Leah's side for a long time. You have been preparing to become her advisor. With her father dead, Leah will become Queen, so you must be ready to take on this responsibility. In times like these strong, responsible men must step forward and protect the realm. That is your duty, as both a wolf and a man," Shane said. Gregory felt pride flow through him, giving him strength. Jack squeezed his shoulder too, giving Gregory that extra boost of support. He nodded solemnly, ready to do anything that Lycanthia needed him to.

"I suggest that the rest of you go home and get some rest. There are going to be troubling days ahead and we will need everyone at their best," Shane said. He sighed and rubbed his temples. Gregory noticed how he was coping with his grief, after all, his son had just died but he was able to carry on, bearing the grief because his son and his granddaughter needed him too. Gregory saw a family in need of a friend. He walked up to Shane and helped him into his chair.

"I will do as you ask. I will not let you down," Gregory said. Shane smiled at him. Gregory suggested that he go in to see Leah, and Shane said that he would in time, once she and Tristan had said all they needed to say to each other.

Then, Gregory turned to Jack, Hank, and Emily, and reiterated Shane's suggestion to go home. "I will come back once I am done with my duties," Gregory said. He could tell that Jack was going to protest, but he took Jack's hand and smiled widely. "Don't worry Jack, it's going to be fine. I won't be long." Jack nodded and walked away with Hank and Emily, while Gregory made his way down into the dungeons.

***

The mood in the castle was somber. The news of Boris' demise had filtered through the castle and left everyone feeling hollow and numb. Two kings in a row had died before their time. Boris' father, Eric von Arnheim, had died to a disease that had claimed the lives of many wolves, including Gregory's own mother. That had been a tragedy, but this, this was an *offense*. To think that someone out there could hate Lycanthia so much they would put Leah in danger and

14

set a trap for the king was inconceivable to Gregory. All his life he had only known peace. Wars and disputes among kingdoms were things from the past, consigned to history, things that he had never had to think about before. But now the shadow loomed over him and seemed to envelop his entire field of vision. His soul screamed with the agony of the grim future, and in the middle of it all was this anguished, impotent whimper, for he could do nothing to change the direction of fate.

And now he was expecting a child. The joy of the unexpected announcement had quickly been extinguished given all that had happened. What life could he possibly give his child if Lycanthia was going to be swallowed into war? What world would his child know? He wouldn't be bringing another life into this world, he would be bringing another soldier, and that thought made the pit of his stomach churn with unease.

Pain throbbed behind Gregory's eyes as he strode down to the dungeon. The guards recognized him and knew that he was a friend of the king's. He announced his intention and the doors were opened. The metal bars scraped across the floor and first Jacques stormed out of his cell. His face was a picture of rage and his body was rigid with tension. His hands were arrows pointed towards the stone floor, and his voice was harrowed.

"I have NEVER been treated like THIS in ALL my life!" he shrieked. "Of all the indignities I have suffered, THIS is the worst of all, and you shall be guaranteed that I am going to give my father a FULL report of all I have suffered here. You call this hospitality?!" he sputtered, and his voice reached an impossibly high pitch that made Gregory tilt his head.

"I will NOT be treated like this and you can be assured there will be recompense needed." He strode out of his cell and lifted his head high, pointing his nose towards the ceiling. "And just for the record, I am rescinding my proposal for the princess' hand. If this is the way Lycanthia treats its guests, then I dare not think of how they treat their citizens! I hope never to see this accursed place again!" Jacques said with a flourish as he strode away from the dungeons as quickly as possible.

Gregory looked at him with a hollow look in his eyes. It was tempting to haul him back and speak spitefully at him, to tell him all that had happened and that, quite frankly, hospitality wasn't at the forefront of their minds when there was a possibility that Jacques and Ferdinand had been in on the plan as well. Instead, Gregory remained quiet. He knew Jacques wouldn't listen to reason and he didn't have the energy to argue with the insufferable man.

"Well, I'm glad that I can finally be free of his incessant moaning," Ferdinand said as he strolled out of the cell and leaned against the stone wall. He picked at his fingernails and seemed relaxed. His red hair drooped over his forehead and wore the same lazy smile that had been on his face from the first moment he had arrived in front of the Queen. Gregory eyed him suspiciously.

"I would have thought you'd have shared his reaction," Gregory said.

Ferdinand shrugged as he cast his gaze around the dungeon. "I must admit that it's not exactly the accommodation I was looking forward to receiving when I arrived in Lycanthia, but I can understand that desperate measures needed to be taken. After all, the princess was in danger. If this was the best way to help her, then so be it. I only wish that I could have helped more. I didn't get a good feeling from Casper from the beginning."

"No?" Gregory asked.

"No, he seemed shifty, and he didn't seem to care about the princess at all. He was quiet, barely saying a word. All he did was glare at everyone. Jacques was a twit, but at least he was good for a joke."

"And you didn't think to mention this to anyone?" Gregory asked.

Ferdinand opened his palms. "What was I to say? Anything I would have said against the other two would have been taken as me trying to sway the princess against my competitors. I thought the best thing to do was keep my own counsel and see where things fell."

"Well, things fell alright. It feels as though the whole world has fallen apart," Gregory said.

"Oh come now, it can't be as bad as all that?" Ferdinand said, crossing his arms across his chest.

"The King is dead. It doesn't get much worse," Gregory leaned forward and his eyes became slits. His voice was a hissed whisper.

"And the princess?"

Gregory softened and regained his usual stance. "Recovering. Thankfully. It's a miracle," he said, and his voice was haunted as he thought of all that had been taken from her. The poison had been negated, but her soul had been purged of something that had been a blessing.

"See, so it's not all bad. As long as the princess recovers and becomes Queen, Lycanthia will still be strong. It seems to me that this plot of Casper's was to rid Lycanthia of the entire royal family and sow chaos, but she survived, and I'm sure they did not count on that."

"No, perhaps not," Gregory said through pursed lips.

"I am sorry for your loss. King Boris was a great man. The world is weaker for his departure," Ferdinand said. The smile finally fell on his face and he looked grave. Gregory offered a thin smile in gratitude.

"Well, you're free to leave now. You can go back to your kingdom and spread the news of the chaos in Lycanthia," Gregory stepped to the side, offering Ferdinand freedom, but the man did not move.

"I don't have any plans to leave yet. After all, I have some unfinished business here," Ferdinand winked at Gregory. Gregory's brow furrowed.

"Surely you don't mean..."

"The Queen will still need a husband, and as far as I can tell I am the last suitor left. It's a shame to win by default. I was hoping to charm the princess myself. I did quite enjoy the reaction to my gambit of offering to take her on a hunt. It certainly made Jacques red with rage as all he could offer her were his precious jewels, but I shall take my victory nonetheless."

Gregory blinked and waited for Ferdinand to laugh, expecting that this was a joke. But Ferdinand did not laugh.

"Surely you jest? This isn't the best time for it."

"No?" Ferdinand challenged. "On the contrary, I believe it is the best time. The Princess has been through a great ordeal. She is going to need someone to support her, someone to lean on, someone to offer hope for the future. In fact, all of Lycanthia is going to need that. The kingdom will be in mourning, but it will also need to look forward with hope to the future. A royal marriage will let them know that the kingdom is in safe hands, and I am more than happy to oblige."

Gregory was skeptical. Was Ferdinand just taking advantage of the circumstances to worm his way into Leah's graces, or was he being genuine? At least one problem had been averted; Leah would not have to hide the fact that she was a wolf.

Ferdinand noted Gregory's silence and closed the distance between the two men. He had an earnest look on his face and spoke to Gregory frankly.

"I know that you do not know me that well. The usual chance for me to introduce myself to Leah has been taken in these unusual times, but I only want the best, and to fulfill the vow I made. Leah has charmed me, and I want to charm her in return. I feel confident that I could make her a good husband, so I would appreciate it if you could arrange for us to meet. I shall be waiting elsewhere in the castle, in more…comfortable accommodations." Ferdinand began to walk away, but he paused before he walked out of Gregory's earshot. "Oh, and one last thing; given what's happened, it might be wise for Lycanthia to have an ally in case the threat of Silvain has not ended. Just something for you to think about."

Gregory would think about it indeed. Ferdinand sauntered away with his hands clasped behind his back, whistling idly as though he hadn't just spent the past few days in a dank dungeon. Gregory was left with much on his mind. He had expected Ferdinand to leave, but instead he had stayed. Was this a show of honor and loyalty, or was it opportunism? If Gregory told Leah of Ferdinand's intentions would be just be letting another kingdom sink its claws into Lycanthia? It was his first duty as the Queen's advisor and it was not an easy one at all. He walked away from the dungeon pondering all that he heard, wishing his heart did not weigh so much.

Chapter Two

The relief Jack felt when Gregory returned had been tempered by the news Gregory brought with him. Then, Leah had returned. It was difficult when triumph and sorrow clashed within a single heart, but these were the feelings that clashed among the entire kingdom. Hank and Emily exchanged worried glances. Shane had remained pensive while Gregory and Tristan had been alone with Leah, and Jack hadn't known what to say at all. When he had returned to Lycanthia he assumed it would be a new beginning, a safe place where he belonged. Instead it was plunged into chaos and nobody knew what the future held.

When it was suggested they get some rest, Jack had begun to protest because he didn't want to leave Gregory's side, but Hank and Emily had pulled him away. They walked away from the castle in silence, not speaking until they returned to Hank's house.

"How are you feeling?" Emily asked. Hank settled on the couch. Jack was numb, but he made some tea for them all, which he hoped would calm their nerves. He used some herbs, like Triss had back in the antiques store, in the hope of giving the tea a little more flavor.

"I'm still in shock. I never thought the king would die like this. Peace has reigned for years. I hadn't even been aware that Silvain had any intention of doing this. It's all so…surreal. And then to think of my Gregory going off with the king and getting caught in a battle. I'm relieved he returned, but I feel sorrow for all those who did not." Hank's words were heavy and he hung his head. Emily glanced at Jack uneasily. She rubbed Hank's broad shoulders and spoke soothing words. The kettle whistled and Jack poured them out some tea. Hank smiled as he brought it over.

"I'm glad the two of you are here. I'd hate to be sitting here in an empty house," he said. Emily smiled, although Jack could tell that there was something on her mind. She had been reluctant to come to Lycanthia in the first place because she had been uneasy about the open secret of Lycanthia and the supernatural elements. Jack had had to convince her, and now he worried that she was going to make her leave.

"I just can't believe this is happening. For so long Lycanthia has been a place of peace, a place that has been different from other places in the world. We've been able to pride ourselves on the fact that we don't suffer from things like war, but that's not true anymore, is it? I'm worried Emily," he said gravely. Emily massaged his shoulders and continued to gaze at Jack with uncertainty. Eventually she patted Hank's shoulders and moved across the room to speak with Jack privately, but he wasn't going to let her tell him that they were leaving.

"Mom, before you say anything please, don't ask me to leave. I can't go. I can't leave Gregory again. I belong here, with him. I know these aren't ideal circumstances, but I need to be here," he said in a strained tone. Emily wore a sad, soft smile and pressed her hand against his arm.

"I would never ask you to do that Jack. I know that you two need to be together. I'm not going to ask you to leave. It's clear that we're needed here," Emily glanced towards Hank. "Besides, I have my own reasons to stay. I can't pretend to say that I understand this all, and I certainly would find it easier if all this wasn't happening, but I don't like seeing people I care about being unhappy. This is all so new to me, but we need to try and be there for them, and each other. Whoever this King of Silvain is, he's not honorable and we can't let him win."

Jack looked at her, stunned and surprised. After everything they had been through it was amazing to hear Emily speak like this, but also unexpected.

"You seem surprised," she laughed lightly. Jack nodded.

"Can you blame me?"

"I suppose not. I've had a lot of time to think about what really happened in Dad's life. At first it was too much for me to accept so I tried to push it away, and when Hank told me the truth, I let my fear get the better of me. But that's not the type of person I want to be Jack. And when I think about it, Hank is exactly the opposite of your father. He lied and cheated and I could never trust him, but Hank opened himself up to me and told me something about himself even though he knew it might have driven me away. I can't ignore that, and I need to let go of my fear because it's only going to stop me from being happy. I do wish your grandfather had been more willing to talk about this place while he was alive though."

"Me too, but looking back on it perhaps we should have seen that there were more to his stories than what we first realized," Jack smiled. Emily hugged him and then returned to Hank, sitting beside him. He perked up when she returned to his side. His hand met hers and they pressed their heads together in a sign of affection. Jack's heart was warmed by this. For so long he had wanted his mother to find happiness again, and now she had. Hank was a good man, although Emily would never have believed that she'd find happiness with a werewolf.

Jack wouldn't have believed it as well. But he had, too, and now he gazed to the window, waiting for Gregory to return.

***

Gregory eventually came back a while later, looking aggrieved and troubled. There were shadows under his eyes and his smile was forced.

"How are you all?" he asked when he walked in.

"How are *you*?" Jack said, rushing to his side. Gregory seemed tired and he shrugged helplessly.

"In all honesty I'm not really sure how I should be feeling. I keep wondering about what's going to happen to Lycanthia, to us. I'm afraid King Stewart isn't going to stop until he has exactly what he wants, and that's an all-out conquest of Lycanthia. I never wanted to bring a child into a world torn by war."

Silence lingered around them. Jack looked down, biting his lip because he didn't know what to say. Sometimes he wished he were older so that he would have a better understanding of what could happen and he could offer better advice. Often he felt alone as a storm raged around him.

It was Hank who rose, and walked towards Gregory, placing his hand on his son's shoulder.

"You have done all of us and all of Lycanthia proud. Your mother would be proud too. I know this is a difficult time for you. It's going to be a difficult time for everyone, but it is a time for the wolves to be strong and to remind the world why they are proud of being exactly who they are, especially with what happened to Leah. You are one of the strongest I have

24

ever known Gregory, and what's more is that you have a good heart. As for your other worries…I know that it is not an ideal time to bring a child into this world, but in truth there is never an ideal time. There are always dangers and uncertainties, but we cannot let those stop us from living our lives. That is how the enemies win. A child can offer hope. It is a sign that we shall not surrender, that we shall not yield. Your child will be taken care of, and be loved. That is all that it needs," Hank said. He clapped Gregory on the shoulder and then urged him to go upstairs to bed, to get some rest because he had been through a lot.

Jack followed.

***

They closed the door behind them and started to peel away their clothes. Gregory sighed with relief when he was naked, and sank into bed, pulling the covers over him. Jack slipped in beside him and smiled when he found the warmth of the man he loved. He nestled in the crook of Gregory's arm, and draped his own arm over Gregory's chest, idly playing with the wiry hair. He sighed as he kissed Gregory's flesh.

"I understand what father was trying to tell me, but it still doesn't sit right with me," Gregory said. "To think of bringing a child into this world when all this is happening…how could anyone be so monstrous? Would we be irresponsible? All I want is for any child of ours to be safe and happy, but if there is a war…"

"We can't let that stop us," Jack said. "I think I understand what Hank was saying. We can't let ourselves be controlled by forces that we can't control. There's nothing we can do about the war, but that doesn't mean we should put our lives on hold."

"I suppose...but on the walk back I have been thinking that perhaps...perhaps it would be better if we left Lycanthia." Gregory's voice caught on his words. Jack gazed wide-eyed at him in shock.

"You can't mean that."

"I do. For our child. I can't do what's best for Lycanthia any longer. I have to think about what's best for our child." He reached around and placed his hand on Jack's abdomen, where inside a life was growing. Jack looked down.

"I understand what you're saying, but Lycanthia is in your blood. It's your home. We can't just forsake it. And what kind of lesson do you want to give to our child? Are we supposed to tell them that it's okay to run away from things that scare you rather than fight for the people you love? That's not the kind of man you are Gregory. This is your home. This is *our* home and there are people who need us, especially Leah."

Gregory nodded sadly. "There's something else. When I freed Ferdinand and Jacques from the dungeon Ferdinand said that he was going to stay around and continue in his efforts to win Leah's hand. He told me to make it clear to her that was not going to be dissuaded by all that has happened. As her advisor I don't know if I should tell her this, or if I should just ignore it and hope that he goes away."

"Why should you want to do that?"

"I don't know if we can trust him Jack. I don't know if he actually cares about Leah, or if he's just using this as an opportunity to seal a marriage pact. What if he's trying to take advantage of Leah? If I'm her advisor then I need to be able to advise, but I don't know how to find my way through the sea of uncertainty."

Jack considered the matter for a moment with a pensive expression on his face. "I'm not sure either. I think you have to look inside and do what you think is best for Leah. Aside from her family you know her better than anyone. That is why she wants you to be her advisor after all. She trusts you Gregory, so you have to trust yourself. If there's nothing else to guide you then at least you can go with your instinct."

Gregory nodded and although he still looked uncertain, he was at least calmed. He tightened his embrace and pulled Jack closer to him. Their naked bodies melted into each other, but the mood in the bed was affectionate and deep rather than filled with lust and passion. It was important in these moments to cling together, to remind themselves what was important in the world.

"It's going to be fine Gregory," Jack said, although he wasn't sure if he believed the words himself. But when he looked up at Gregory, he found that his belief strengthened. "I know this isn't the way we wanted our lives to turn out, but as long as we have each other we'll be fine. And just to add to the praise, I'm proud of you for what you did as well, and I'm glad that you returned."

Gregory nodded in thanks. "I wish I was not the only one," he said.   He closed his eyes. Jack let out a short breath, thinking of the wolves that had lost their lives on that fateful day, including King Boris. There were small scratches and scars that had not fully healed yet on Gregory's body. Jack traced some of these with his fingers. Gregory murmured that it was a pleasing sensation, and a smile played on his face as he fell asleep. Jack watched him slip into slumber and he caressed Gregory's face, kissing it lightly, before falling into the pillow himself and sleeping. As he did so his hand fell upon his stomach, as though to cradle his child, and he thought about the future. His mind was split in two. In one the future was bright and bold. He and Gregory ran through a field of spring flowers swinging a child between them. The air was filled with gleeful laughter and birds chirped happily. The other possibility was a bleak world, with crumbled buildings and shadows spilling over the ground. Jack was alone, holding a weeping child.

Chapter Three

Gregory's heart was still unsettled despite all the wisdom and kind words bestowed upon him by the people around him. He tried to think of the best possible future for himself and his family, but it was difficult when there was so much uncertainty around him. In some ways he wished that Silvain would just attack and get all this over with so that they could move on. The tension was bitter in his heart, and an anxious knot twisted like a knife in his stomach.

He awoke feeling hungry, although the food that was presented to him was bland. There was much on his mind and he knew that he could not delay in speaking to Leah for too long about Ferdinand as the situation would only grow more difficult to deal with. He could tell that Jack was worried; they all were really. Gregory wished he could say or do more to help alleviate their fears, but it was so, so difficult. When he stepped outside the air in Lycanthia was sweet and warm. For a moment he closed his eyes and inhaled deeply, and he was able to forget about all his troubles. Inevitably, however, they came rushing in again and only served to form a cloud around his mind. He shuffled towards the castle. Even walking seemed to take more of an effort today.

The castle was surrounded by mourners, as was the custom in Lycanthia. They would hold a vigil for King Boris until the funeral. They were on their knees, murmuring prayers for the departed King. Gregory stepped carefully through them until he was in the castle. The mood was still grim and shadows seemed to lurk everywhere. The faces of guards and servants were all grave and a deathly silence hung in the air. He walked up to Leah's room and walked in to see Tristan sitting beside her. His face was pale and shadows hung under his eyes. He looked as though he had not slept at all.

"Have you been here all night?" Gregory asked.

Tristan nodded. "I wanted to stay with her, to make sure that nothing would happen, that nothing had gone wrong," Tristan said, looking down at his daughter with worry etched upon his face.

"And did it?"

"No," Tristan said. "She has rested well." He sighed heavily. "I suppose I should get some rest myself."

"Yes, you should. Leah is going to need you," Gregory said. Tristan rose, albeit reluctantly, and walked over towards Gregory. He looked Gregory straight in the eyes and smiled in earnest.

"She is going to need you too, and we are lucky to have you. You have always been a good friend to her Gregory, and I'm glad that you're here to help her through this. I hope you know that you can count on our help as well with anything you need. I know that what's happened has overshadowed some recent events, but none of us have forgotten about the miracle that is your child. We shall do everything we can to help protect Jack," Tristan said.

There was a look of surprise on Gregory's face as he nodded and thanked Tristan for the kind words. The fact that Tristan took the time to speak to him about this meant the world to Gregory. In truth he had never been sure how Leah's parents felt about him. Sometimes he assumed they merely tolerated his presence because he was Leah's friend. He wasn't noble after all, so he didn't really have a place in the castle, but it seemed they actually did value him.

"There's something else as well," Tristan said. "I just wanted to thank you personally for coming back with the news, and for being with Boris when he died. I know that it must have been a relief for him to know that you had escaped and would make it back here. I'm sure it would have made him feel that he died for something. It would have been a heroic death, and that is at least a small mercy."

Gregory nodded as Tristan placed a hand on his shoulder and squeezed it tightly before he left. Gregory moved around to sit by Leah's side. She looked so peaceful. The wound on her shoulder looked far less harrowing now. The dark skin had receded and the wound was no longer festering. After a few moments of sitting there her eyes fluttered and she awakened. She still looked weak, but after some rest she looked more like herself and pushed herself into a sitting position.

"Good morning Gregory," she said. Speaking was still an effort for her, but her breathing was not as labored as it had been when she was first revived.

"You're looking better," he said, smiling.

"I wish I felt it." She raised a hand to her head. "My head still throbs and I feel nauseous all the time, as though I'm going to spill my guts at a moment's notice. I don't know if it's the aftereffects of the poison or grief, or a mixture of both," she said grimly.

"I'm sure that it will pass soon," he said. After Leah had massaged her temples for a few moments she reached down and clasped Gregory's hand, squeezing it tightly.

"Thank you for everything you did for me Gregory. You are a true friend. I couldn't ask for a better friend." Her smile was radiant and even though she had lost the wolf essence, she had lost none of her beauty.

"Thank you Leah, but I'm sorry I wasn't there on that first night to protect you."

"Nobody could have foreseen what Casper did. I don't think there was any way I could avoid it. Besides, you were elsewhere." A playful look appeared in her eyes. "Father told me that you had some special news to share with me. He said that Jack came back. Are the two of you officially official now?"

"I think we're a little more than that," Gregory chuckled. Leah tilted her head to the side and crinkled her brow, indicating that he should elaborate. "Well," he said, taking a deep breath. "It turned out that Jack wasn't just a tourist here. His grandfather actually came from Lycanthia. He was one of us in fact, but he wanted to be free of the wolf, so he sought out the Chalice of Sinterbaum and became human, and then left for America. But he told stories of this place. And I guess something of the wolf remained inside him because Jack and I... We're...expecting a child." A smile spread across his face when he said this, and he still couldn't quite believe it.

"A child?!" Leah gasped. She clasped both of Gregory's hands in her own and looked delighted. "Oh Gregory, this is most wonderful and most unexpected! A child...just like me. You know, it's going to need someone who knows what it's like to have two fathers," she lowered her voice and winked at him.

"I don't think there's anyone we'd rather have as the baby's godmother," Gregory said with a laugh. "But there's a long way to go until then."

"It'll pass by quickly. Oh Gregory, I am so happy for you and Jack. This is wonderful news. It seems as though you have everything you ever wanted. And to think, I used to tease you for wanting to fall in love like this."

"I always told you that you should have had more faith," Gregory said. Leah smiled, but then the smile faded from her face. He had been thinking about the matter with Ferdinand during his journey to the castle and he still hadn't come to a decision, but now that he was in Leah's presence, he knew what he had to do.

"Leah, there's something I need to talk with you about. When I was in the dungeon yesterday, I spoke with Ferdinand and he still expresses an interest in courting you."

"He does?" Leah's ears pricked up and a slight blush appeared on her cheeks. "Even in my current state?"

"He does. I was unsure whether to tell you this or not because I can't be certain that he has yours or Lycanthia's best interests at heart. It could be that he is merely using this as an opportunity to stake a claim on your affections when you are most vulnerable."

"Is that what you truly think, or is that what you fear?" Leah asked. It was an intriguing question. Gregory thought back to his interactions with Ferdinand and stroked his chin.

"I think it is a genuine concern just because the world is clearly not what we thought it was. Having said that, Ferdinand could easily have left, but he chose to stay. He does seem to have a unique outlook on current events and despite everything that has happened you are still going to need a king."

Leah nodded. "I suppose I am," she sighed. "In truth that is the last thing on my mind. Perhaps I should be grateful that there is anyone still willing to marry me given what happened. I do not feel much of a queen at the moment," she pouted and her face fell, turning ashen. "After my father's funeral I shall meet with him and we shall talk. It will be good to get to know him, and I can judge his intentions for myself."

"As you wish. And for the record, anyone would be lucky to marry you."

Leah laughed darkly. "I have been scarred and I am half of myself."

"But you are still you. Even I can see that," Gregory tried to remain positive. He wanted to convince her that she could still have a good life, but when she looked up at him her eyes were liquid and her sadness was so deep, he could have drowned in it.

"Then you are blind," she said. "Gregory, I know you are trying to reassure me and that is very sweet of you, but I have had enough of that from my family. As much as they try to understand they cannot. It feels as though something has been ripped from me, torn from my heart," she jabbed outstretched fingers into her ribcage. "I've lost a part of myself and I can never get it back." Her voice trembled with emotion. "I keep searching for it inside, but there's nothing there, just emptiness, just…nothing." Her head lolled to the side and her hand fell into her lap. She looked desolate and forlorn.

"I wish there was something else to be done. If I could transfer my essence to you I would, in a heartbeat," Gregory said. Leah shook her head.

"Thank you, but I could never ask anyone to do that. Having lost it myself…I could never put anyone else through that. It's as though something deep and profound is missing from my soul. I'm not sure I will ever get used to it, and what's worse is that it is the thing that connected me so deeply with my father. Not only have I lost him, but I lost what we shared as well."

Gregory pursed his lips. "You are still the Wolf Queen. I'm sure that the pack will still embrace you. You may have lost the ability to shift into a wolf, but that doesn't mean everything in your heart has changed."

"The rules are the rules Gregory," Leah said with a sad smile. "And that leads to the other thing I need to talk with you about. Father and I had a long conversation yesterday about the state of Lycanthia and how to handle things moving forward. There is still the matter of the wolves. For generations, the king or queen has also led the wolves. It is a tradition that I must break."

"No," Gregory gasped.

"Yes," Leah insisted. "You know it must be this way Gregory. How can I lead the pack when I am not one of you? It isn't fair. It isn't right. The pack needs a leader who can shift into a wolf, and that is where you come in."

"Me?" Gregory asked, furrowing his brow.

"Yes Gregory, you," Leah laughed. "I can think of nobody better to lead the pack now. You are still connected with the crown, and you have been my most trusted friend. You were also trusted by my father. There is nobody more suited, and at the next gathering I will make it official."

"But...but..." Gregory said, floundering as he tried to search for a reason why he shouldn't be the leader of the wolves. "I'm too young. They'd never accept me."

"Of course they will, and youth has nothing to do with these. Besides, you are going to have a wolf child with Jack. That counts for a lot as well. Please Gregory, do this for me. I want to know that the pack is in the hands of someone I trust. There are going to be troubling times ahead and the transition needs to be a smooth one. The crown and the pack must be united, and with you leading them I know that it will be. Who knows, this may begin a new generation where the wolf pack has a leader of its own, one separate from the crown. This could be the beginning of a new lineage, one continuing with your child."

"I am honored," Gregory bowed his head. "That is if we make it through these troubled times."

Leah brushed her hand against Gregory's arm. "We will. Lycanthia has stood against greater foes than the King of Silvain. He tried to poison me and I survived. We can stand against anything he throws at us. The guards are preparing defenses in case we are attacked, and it is you who must prepare the wolves for the same thing. Now that we know he threatens us he has lost all his advantage. The only boon he had was surprise, and he wasted it on attacking me. When he comes for us again, we shall be ready for him." Her determined tone belied her weakened state. Her eyes blazed with anger and her hand clenched into a tight ball. Gregory was inspired by her show of strength and he hoped that he could offer some semblance of this strength when he addressed the wolves.

To think…leader of the wolves. It was a position he had never coveted or craved. In truth it wasn't something he had ever considered for himself, but he would do the duty his Queen asked of him.

"The days ahead will be busy, but we cannot lose sight of what makes Lycanthia special," Leah said. "Gregory, we have spent a great deal of time discussing what we would do when we were older and I was Queen and you were my advisor. Things may not have developed exactly as we pictured them, but we are older now, and the future has found us earlier than we believed it would. It is time for us to grow now, to become the adults that we were always meant to be. Lycanthia needs us." She reached out her hand and opened her palm. Gregory stared at it for a moment, and then clutched it tightly. With that gesture they sealed a bond that would last a lifetime, a sacred promise to take care of the kingdom together, both the mortal side, and the wolf side.

Gregory wasn't entirely sure what had happened, only that he felt a greater weight on his shoulders than before, but he was ready for this. He *was* ready.

Chapter Four

It took a couple of days for King Boris' funeral to be arranged. All of Lycanthia gathered in the castle's courtyard. Jack was standing beside Gregory near the front, a privileged view for an outsider, although he wasn't sure that being an outsider was an accurate label any longer. Leah had not made a full recovery, but she was looking healthier and seemed to be returning to the girl that Jack had met briefly. When he looked at her he thought about how she had had something precious stolen from her. He had always imagined what it would have been like for his grandfather to let go of the wolf inside, but at least it was something he wanted. Leah had had it ripped away because it was the only way to save her. She'd had no choice, and he wondered what it must have felt inside. His hand instinctively fell to his stomach as he wondered if it would have been similar to having his child taken away from him. The thought filled him with revulsion and he knew he would never have been able to survive that. He hoped that Leah could find peace now that she was a mortal.

She stood on a throne at the top of the courtyard, flanked by her father and grandfather. The crowd of Lycanthia stood beside her; a crown that had been made especially for her. It was smaller than the one that her father wore. In front of her was a large bowl, and in this bowl burned a grand fire, like the flame of Olympus. It crackled and danced with vibrant energy, churning and writhing with heat. Thick smoke rose through the air, and it caught everyone's attention. The crowd spanned the entire courtyard, and even spilled outside.

Leah remained silent while Tristan stepped forward. His voice was filled with grief. Jack was close enough to see his lip tremble. He had already been to too many funerals, and hoped that it would be the last one for a good while.

"We come together today to say goodbye to King Boris von Arnheim, Lycanthia's protector. He died for the realm, a realm he always loved," Tristan gazed into the flame, as though he was gazing upon Boris' face. "From the first moment I saw him I knew he was a special man, and we devoted our lives to each other. He took his responsibilities as a king seriously and never wavered in his devotion to the realm. He learned his lessons from his father well, and attempted to do his best to impart them on his daughter.

These are dark days for Lycanthia. The threat of Silvain cannot be understated, but I know one thing to be true; if we live by Boris' example then Lycanthia will never fall. Through his life he showed strength, love, and compassion. He watched over the realm as it grew to ever greater heights of prosperity and he had everyone's best intentions at heart. Today we say goodbye to a fine King, one who will long live in the hearts and minds of everyone who knew him."

Tristan almost collapsed into sobs as he finished his eulogy, but managed to step back without losing his footing. Leah then rose and walked towards the flame. She picked up a golden rod that ended in a deep scoop. There was a bucket of water next to the flame.

"As the King's daughter and heir to his throne, it is my duty to extinguish the flame of his life. Take a moment to remember my father as he would want to be remembered, as a loving king who only ever wanted the best for Lycanthia. I will try my very best to live up to the example he set, but I know I will never surpass him as King. Goodbye father. We love you."

There were murmurs in the crowd as people said their goodbyes. Some were whispered, some were yelled, while others were silent thoughts that were kept secret. Jack's lips remained sealed, but he heard Gregory and Hank whisper things either side of him. Lycanthia was united in their mourning of the King and it was a profound thing to witness. It was a stark contrast to his grandfather's funeral, which had only been attended by a handful of people. Jack wondered what his own funeral would be like, although he quickly pushed away the thought as it made him shudder.

After a few moments where everyone had had their chance to say a goodbye, Leah scooped water out of the bucket and doused the flames. The water hissed and thick clouds of smoke billowed out. Gregory had explained the ritual to Jack before the funeral so that he knew what to expect. The flame represented the life that had been lost, and the smoke that escaped represented the soul rising to heaven. The flame was so big that it took Leah a few motions to put it out fully, and the smoke rose in a huge plume. Jack's lips parted as he watched the flames flicker and die out, the last signs of a life. All in attendance watched in silence as the smoke rose into the air and dissipated, leaving behind nothing but memories.

Emotions ran high as Tristan stepped forward again. He picked up the crown. Leah had returned to her seat.

"As the cycle of life turns, so must we. As one reign ends, another must begin. The duty of protecting and ruling Lycanthia now falls onto Queen

Leah. The King is Dead. Long live the Queen." Tristan said these words as he placed the golden crown upon Leah's head. Applause and cheers emanated from the crowd. Grief turned to anticipation and celebration as they welcomed back their queen, who had been so near to death. She rose and held up her arms, as though to embrace her royal subjects. Jack watched on in awe, and knew that he was in the right place. Nothing like this would ever have happened in America.

***

After Leah had been crowned, she sat on the throne. People were given the chance to walk up and greet her, as well to pay their respects to the great flame that had been extinguished. Jack waited and watched as the commoners walked forward first, bowing to their new queen. Leah smiled at them all and thanked them for their kind words, gestures, and attendance. She was a humble queen and it was an attitude that would serve her well in the years to come, as long as Silvain didn't destroy Lycanthia as they so wished.

Jack squeezed Gregory's hand and his gaze fell upon a few different faces. Ferdinand waited patiently for his chance to greet the queen.

"I hope that I didn't make a mistake in advising her to speak with him," Gregory said.

"I'm sure it'll be fine. I know I don't know her as well as you do, but I don't think she's the type to give her heart to someone who isn't worthy," Jack said.

"No, that's true," Gregory seemed reassured by his comment. Then, Jack approached a familiar face. Triss dabbed her eyes and sniffed as she gazed at the flame, and she seemed to be waiting for a chance to get near Shane.

"I'm glad to see you here," Jack said.

"I wouldn't miss it for the world. Boris was such a sweet boy, and he turned into a wonderful man. I'm as proud of him as though he were my own child," she said. In a way Boris was. Jack remembered the story Triss had told him, of how she had had to pretend to be Boris' mother so that Shane and Eric's secret wouldn't be revealed. That seemed a long time ago now. Thankfully, Jack and Gregory wouldn't have to go through anything like that.

"I'm sorry for your loss," Jack said.

Triss smiled. "Thank you. I just wish that I had had a chance to see him again. It had been so long. You always intend to do something else, to see people again, but then time slips away from you all too easily. There's never enough time in the world. Never," she said. "But how are you doing? Do you feel more settled now that you're back in Lycanthia?"

"I do," Jack smiled, and glanced towards Gregory. "It's perfect being here, with him. Even Mom is happier. I think we'd be a little less uneasy if things weren't happening as they are, but despite that there's no place we'd rather be."

"I'm glad to hear it. It's always a good thing when you can discover the place you're meant to be. You're a lucky man Jack," she leaned in for a hug and kissed him on the cheek. Emily seemed intrigued by this as she had never met Triss before, so her and Hank came over. Hank of course did recognize her. There was a moment of amusement as Emily had to catch up and understand who Triss was. Jack made the introductions and they enjoyed getting to know each other until it was their time to pass by the extinguished flame and pay their respects to the departed king and the newly crowned Queen.

Jack watched on with interest as Ferdinand took his place before the Queen. From what Gregory had described, Ferdinand was a cocky young man with confidence and charm flowing from every pore. But he did not look like that now. Now, he seemed respectful and dignified. He bowed his head and placed his hand on his heart when he approached the empty bowl. Although Jack could not hear what he said to Leah, he seemed to say the right thing as a genuine smile appeared upon her face, and that was a welcome sight indeed.

Then, it became time for Jack and Gregory to walk up. A solemn feeling filled Jack's heart as they walked up to the ornate bowl. It smelled of smoke and ash, making his eyes cloudy with tears. He mourned the king, although not with as much intensity as the people of Lycanthia because he had only known Boris briefly, and had not had too many personal interactions with him. But he knew how much the King had meant to the people of Lycanthia, and also to the wolves. Jack took in as much as he could because it was a part of his new heritage, and when the time came, he wanted to be able to explain this to his son or daughter. It was an historic moment, and he wanted to take as much of it in as he could.

When he approached Leah, he could see that she was still weary and no doubt the emotional toll of the day would weigh her down even more heavily. She was doing well at displaying strength, even though she was still weak. It must have been hard for her as she was mourning something else as well, the loss of her wolf essence. Jack bowed along with Gregory.

Leah smiled at them. She turned to Jack, as she had already said everything she needed to say to Gregory.

"I hear that congratulations are in order," she said, her eyes twinkling. Jack smiled.

"Thank you, your Grace," Jack replied. Leah rolled her eyes.

"Oh please, I get that enough from other people. I don't need that from family."

"Family?" Jack asked, uneasily.

"Of course! You and Gregory are family, especially if I'm going to be godmother to your child," Leah smile genuinely, and it was infectious. "Today is a sad day, but it is important for us to look to the future and think of all the good that awaits us. Your child reminds us what all this is for. Life should not be defined by death. I look forward to speaking to your more about this. Thank you for coming today; I'm sure that my father would appreciate it."

Jack smiled and said that he was sure she would be a good Queen. He had no evidence to back that up of course, other than what was in his own heart. They walked away to allow the next person to speak to her, and returned home, leaving the crowd behind.

***

Once they were at home, they relaxed in chairs and had some food, although eating was an act done more out of habit than anything else. It wasn't really a day when appetites were at their peak.

"It was a lovely service," Emily said. She had said the same thing at Michael's funeral. It seemed to be one of those stock phrases that people used to fill the silence and make things a little less awkward.

"Yes, it was. Usually the body is placed in the flame as well, but I suppose that wasn't possible this time. It makes my blood boil to think of the King's body being left torn and broken in Maugrim's Pass. Or worse, taken back to Silvain," Hank said.

"You don't think they really would do that?" Gregory gasped.

"Why not?" Hank replied gruffly. "They haven't shown any respect for us so far. Why would they treat the king like he meant anything?"

It was a question that none of them could answer and the possibilities were terrifying. The thought of Silvain loomed over them like a shadow, and made the future bleak. After spending some time together, Gregory and Jack left to be by themselves.

"Do you know what you're going to say to them?" Jack asked.

Gregory sighed. "I honestly have no idea. I'm still not sure if this is something I can even do. I never thought of myself as a leader."

"I'm sure you never thought of yourself as a father too, but life has a funny way of giving us things we never expected," Jack teased. Gregory smiled and the tension seemed to slip away from his shoulders.

"I just wish I had a better grasp on things. I'm sure there are other people who are more suited to be a leader than I am. I hope that nobody holds it against me."

"I'm sure they won't. And I'm sure you'll be fine. I just wish I could come. I could offer them a personal testimony on why I think you'd make a good leader."

"I think you're a little biased," Gregory said, leaning in towards Jack. Gregory wrapped his arm around Jack's neck and pulled him in for a kiss. Jack let the warm sensations run through him. The tingling was a nice break from the melancholy that had run through his heart at the funeral.

"Maybe I am, but I wouldn't want to be anything else when it comes to you," he said, kissing Gregory back. Their love burned intensely even though it was a somber day. Jack remembered the last time he had been at a funeral; after his grandfather had died Jack had returned home and sat alone for a while, trying to understand why people had to die and how he was going to process his sorrow. Now he could be with Gregory and they could share their grief. It made it more palatable, although he was still worried for the future and what being the leader of the wolves meant for Gregory. In Jack's mind a leader meant somebody was going to lead them into battle, and given the situation with Silvain it seemed that a battle was entirely likely. It had already been heart-wrenching to wait for Gregory to return from a negotiation with the Silvainians. Jack didn't want to think about what it would be like to have to wait for him to come back to battle.

And yet he also knew that it would have been unfair of him to ask Gregory to refuse this request. Jack knew how important it was to be a wolf, how it was such a part of his identity. It would be a part of their child's identity as well, and Jack would have to cope with the fact that it was a part of life he could never truly understand or be a part of.

When Gregory and Hank left for the meeting, Jack remained with his mother and she came beside him to offer him her sympathy.

"What's on your mind?" Emily asked.

Jack sighed. "Actually, I was just thinking about the state of Lycanthia now compared to when grandfather left. They didn't have these meetings then. I wonder if he still would have wanted to get rid of the wolf inside him if he had been part of a pack like Gregory and Hank."

"I don't know. I suppose he might have felt like he was a part of something bigger, but it's lucky for us that he did leave otherwise I would never have been born, and we wouldn't be standing here right now," Emily said. She cupped Jack's head in her hands and pulled his forehead down, rising on her tiptoes to kiss him. It was something she had done throughout his life, but as he had grown, she had to make more effort to be able to display her affection in this way. Despite everything that had happened, he was still her little boy. Even though he was pregnant and expecting a child of his own.

Chapter Five

Night had drawn in and the secrets of Lycanthia snuck out from their hiding holes. The day had been lined with sorrow, and it was not over yet. The stars twinkled upon a black blanket, and the moon was pale and full. As Gregory looked up at it, he couldn't shake the feeling it was sad, as though it wept for the lost king, and for the sorrow that plagued Lycanthia.

"Are you ready?" Hank asked as they walked away from their home, turning down the streets that led to the shadowed forests.

"I'm not sure," Gregory said. He summoned courage and tried to be the kind of man that could be ready for this kind of thing, but it was entirely difficult and he wasn't sure if he could actually be the person Leah thought he could be. Hank clamped a hand on his shoulder.

"Your mother would be so proud of you now, and I'm proud of you too. To think...my son...leader of the wolves."

"I'm still not sure if they're going to accept me. I'm hardly the strongest," Gregory said.

"No, that is true, but you are wise. You know, when you were younger you hardly said a word. You were so quiet that I thought there was actually something wrong with you. I was convinced that we had to take you to a healer, but your mother, bless her soul, told me that you were just listening. That's what you've done all your life; you've listened, and you've based your actions on what you've heard rather than charging in. That's something that will stand you in good stead. You're well-liked among the wolves and I'm sure none of them will say anything against you. If they do, they'll have to get through me," Hank nodded and puffed out his chest with pride. Gregory grinned widely, although it felt like there was much he needed to say to his father.

"Father, I wanted to apologize. I know I'm not the son that you wanted. I know that you would have preferred me to find a life on the sea like you did. I'm sorry I haven't followed in the family trade." It was an unspoken tension that had been present between the two men for a long time. Having been to a funeral that day, Gregory was filled with an urge to express these troubles that had been weighing on his mind. He knew that there had been many things left unsaid between Leah and Boris. She would never get a chance to tell him any of those things now. Gregory understood how swiftly life could be taken away. When he closed his eyes there was a throbbing in his mind. The darkness was filled with images of flying arrows, echoes of men's death howls, and then the king being swarmed by the enemy. Terror tasted bitter. It tasted like blood.

He was pulled from his thoughts by Hank's gentle words.

"You don't have to apologize for that. Yes, I would have loved it if you had expressed an interest in fishing so it could be something that we shared, but you know, one thing you'll learn when your child grows up is that they're not just mini versions of you. You have a mind of your own and desires of your own. I would never have wanted you to do something you would have hated. Everyone has to find their own path in life. It would all be boring if we just did the same thing as our parents without listening to what is in our hearts. I am proud of the path you have taken, as would your mother be." His face broke out in a grin. "Besides, the joy of having a grandchild is that I can try to make up for the mistakes I made with you. Don't think for a second that I'm not going to be taken the baby out on the sea with me the first chance I get," he winked, and then added, "plus Jack has shown a lot of interest and an aptitude for the sea as well. I don't think my legacy is going to end with you."

Gregory did find this reassuring. He hated to think he had been a disappointment to his father, but Hank was right when he said there were other possibilities. Gregory thought to the future and wondered what his child would be like. It helped to alleviate his trauma from the slaughter in Maugrim's Pass. His conversations with Jack and Leah had helped him to come to terms with the fact that he couldn't let the dark world extinguish the flame of life. His baby was a symbol of hope, and he had to use that for his strength rather than let his fear define him.

With that having been said and with these thoughts strong in his mind, Gregory was able to stride forward and meet his destiny. He glanced at his father.

"Ready to race?" he asked, and as soon as the question was out of his mouth he shifted into a wolf and felt all the primal energy and vigor surging through him. The air tasted tangy on his tongue and it flowed through his thick fur. His feet padded against the ground as he left the path and ventured into the dark woods, making his own path, led by his instincts and experience. The primal energy was a release for him, a way to process his turbulent emotions. Everything seemed simpler when he was a wolf. He loved Jack. He hated the Silvainians. He was proud to lead the wolves. These emotions were pure and distilled into their most basic, powerful essence. Everything was made crystal clear for him. The doubts and fears were chased away by the strength of his wolf mind, and he felt invincible.

***

When he reached the clearing where the gathering took place he shifted back into a human. His wide, panting jaw and lolling tongue turned into laughter as he waited for Hank to catch up. Hank had been a few paces behind him.

"That's not fair! You didn't give me a chance!" Hank protested. Gregory shrugged and enjoyed the feeling of adrenaline surging through his body. But then he looked across at the clearing and saw Leah sitting on a fallen log. She looked so small and pensive, unlike how she usually was. She wore a white gown that made her look like a child of the moon. It was inlaid with small gems that sparkled and glittered as it caught the moonlight. His heart sank as he realized again that she had lost the ability to feel something so simple.

Hank nodded to him and went his own way, speaking to some of his friends. There was much to speak of, of course, for although they had all mourned King Boris von Arnheim at the funeral, they had only mourned his human half. Now it was time to say goodbye to the Wolf King.

A lot of the wolves were still in human form, although some had been unable to help themselves and shifted already. The stars were visible in the clear sky and the grass danced as it was caught by the gentle night breeze. Old stones stood and Gregory stopped for a moment to look around at this most ancient place, thinking about all the wolves who had stood here before. Then, he walked up to Leah, who smiled as he approached.

"How are you?" he asked.

"I'm…as good as I can be," she said. "It's strange being here. I used to feel a connection to this place but now…" her face dropped and she pursed her lips. "I suppose we should get on with proceedings."

"Wait, how are you after the funeral? What did Ferdinand say to you?"

"Oh," Leah smiled. "Just a little joke. He really is quite charming. I was thinking that perhaps we could take a little walk somewhere, Ferdinand and I, and you and Jack. I think it would be good for you to get to know him."

"That sounds like a wonderful idea," Gregory said. Then he could tell for certain whether Ferdinand was genuine in his wish to be Leah's consort, or if this was just a cruel grab for power.

"I'm going to miss these," Leah said, looking up and out towards the clearing. Her eyes glistened with sorrow.

"You can still attend. I'm sure that nobody here would object."

Leah dismissed the idea with a single shake of her head. "No, I cannot allow that to happen. We have our rules for a reason and there can be no exceptions, for one exception will only lead to another. This is my last gathering Gregory, and I have made my peace with that." She squeezed his hand gently as she rose and then walked into the clearing, raising her voice to get everyone's attention.

"Today I was crowned Queen of Lycanthia," she began in a regal tone. "Usually that would mean I become Queen of the Wolves as well, as had been tradition for generations. But these are strange times we live in, and much is changing. I'm sure you are all aware of what happened with the Silvainian plot to tear the royal family asunder. They poisoned me, but still I live!" she raised her fist, and there were cheers and barks erupting from the crowd. "However, in order to save me the wolf inside me needed to die." The cheers faded. "I can no longer be your Queen, as much as it pains me to say it. My father was a good man and always proud of his heritage. He taught me how to cherish being a wolf and how to best serve you. He taught me that Lycanthia cannot thrive unless the natural and supernatural parts are in harmony, and that is what I seek to maintain. I respect the rules of tradition and after tonight I shall not attend a gathering again, so I need to leave you with a strong and capable leader, someone I trust with your lives and with the safety of Lycanthia. I leave you with Gregory."

She stepped aside, allowing Gregory to step forward. There was a lump in his throat and he wasn't entirely sure what to say. The gathered crowd looked at him expectantly. He glanced towards Leah, who gave him an encouraging nod, and then in the crowd he spied his father. Gregory drew strength from him.

"I know these unexpected turns of events are going to take some time to fully process and understand. We are all in a state of shock about what happened, but one thing I've learned is that we cannot afford ourselves the time when there is an enemy out there," he pointed in the general direction of Silvain. "They want to tear Lycanthia to pieces. They want to rid the world of us, and I am not going to let them succeed." When he started speaking the words came through his mind as though they had a life of their own. His blood tingled and his voice grew deeper with a commanding authority.

"Here we stand, on the ground where our ancestors stood. They gave us life and taught us all the lessons that we adhere to today. We are a proud race and we cannot allow this enemy to win. In a hundred years I want our own descendants to stand here proudly, remembering this time when Lycanthia was defended. I want songs to be sung and stories to be told about our glory. I have seen the evil tactics used by this Silvainian king. He sent his own son into our kingdom under false pretenses to attack our Queen, and then he lured our King out and slaughtered our men. We will make him pay for these crimes. He cannot hope to hide behind silver. With the help of the human guards we shall fight off this threat when it comes, and stand true for Lycanthia."

"For Lycanthia!" A ringing cheer sounded, and goosebumps appeared on Gregory's arms. He waited for them to fade before he spoke again.

"But that is for the future. In the coming days you must look into your hearts and find your fighting spirit. You must think about the gifts that have been left to you through your bloodline. We are fighting for our home, for honor, and for the generations to come," he thought about his own child and this gave his words an even more fervent energy. "But now we must mourn our fallen King," he glanced towards Leah, "and the wolf spirit that has been taken from our Queen."

In that instant he shifted into a wolf. All those who had not yet shifted also embraced the wolf essence and soon Leah was the only human left among a pack of wolves. They lifted their jaws to the moon and let out a chorus of howls. The powerful animalistic wails melted together, creating a cacophony that blanketed the entire clearing and must have been heard in Lycanthia. Gregory hoped that it could be heard in Silvain as well, and that the evil kingdom would know that the wolves were ready to defend themselves, ready to coat the ground of Lycanthia in blood if it was necessary.

When the howling was over and Gregory had shifted back into a man, Leah thanked him and hugged him tightly.

"You're going to do just fine. You're a natural," she said, kissing him on the cheek before she departed and returned to the castle. Gregory had to admit that he felt strong, with a kind of vigor that he had never really felt before. The wolves came up to him and welcomed him as the leader of their pack. Some of them had concerns, which he reassured, or questions, which he answered. Many of them also wanted to know exactly what had happened in Maugrim's Pass, so he sat them down and told them the story, which lasted long into the night.

***

It had been one of the more intense gatherings that Gregory had ever been a part of, and that was to be expecting given the circumstances. If any of the wolves had had doubts about Gregory when Leah announced him as their new leader, there were none remaining by the time the gathering had disbanded. The wolves returned to their lives with much on their mind, for they all took Gregory's words to heart and thought about how far they were willing to go to defend Lycanthia and fight for its future.

Gregory was filled with something else as well. Because of the emotional turmoil of the last few days there had been something burning inside him, something simmering under the surface, but there had been so many other things to worry about he hadn't actually been able to release it. But now he could feel it beginning to erupt, wanting to be free, and it seemed the appropriate time. Now that he had accepted his role as leader of the wolf pack, he had a newfound confidence and this imbued him with crackling energy that could not be contained. There was only one place he wanted to be and one person he wanted to be with, so as soon as the gathering was over he raced home, sprinting through the forest, ignoring the branches that whipped him and crashed through the door, shifting back into a man.

He bounded up the stairs and flung open the door to his bedroom. Jack was there, in bed, waiting for him. He spoke to greet Gregory, but Gregory had no words. He was a man of passion, of instinct, of desire. He was done with feeling complicated emotions and grief. All he wanted was something pure, to bathe in the body of the man he loved. He tore off the sheet of the bed, exposing Jack's body. Then, he threw himself onto the bed. His strong arms spread over Jack's body like vines, his hands roamed every inch of that perfect flesh. Gregory was like a mindless beast with only one intention; to take and to please, to claw and bit and growl with hot intensity. His kiss was like fire and he suffocated Jack's moans. His eyes glowed with passion as he pinned Jack to the bed and started to peel away his clothes. He was only wearing light clothes during the warm Lycanthian nights, and they offered no resistance to Gregory's relentless ardor.

The stifled moans and terse gasps were a cacophony around Gregory's mind as he pulled off his own clothes. Jack's hands were responsive and mirrored Gregory's hunger. Gregory grunted as he felt Jack's hands running around his torso, through the thick bed of hair, pulling down to where the hair thinned into a single line that led to the hot, masculine part of his body.

There was no time for sweet whisperings, no time for vows of affection or promises of love. They both needed a rampant release of emotion. Hot tears stung Gregory's eyes as it was so overwhelming that he could not contain any of his emotions. They all flowed out of him in a blistering torrent, a surge of fire that might as well have been dragon's breath.

The bed creaked as they rolled around. Their bodies were slick with sweat. Hot breaths beat against the air. It felt as though a hundred hands writhed over his skin. Gregory didn't know where he ended and Jack began.

He gripped Jack in a tight embrace. A searing kiss bruised their lips and their tongues danced with each other. The sweet taste lingered as Gregory pushed Jack to the bed. Jack's arms splayed out either side of him and his head lolled to the side, overwhelmed by the frantic and intense burst of passion. Gregory slithered over his body, pressing his weight against Jack's skin. He tasted the slick sweat and the musky aroma of masculinity and sex. He knew all the sweet spots that could drive Jack crazy, and his fingers darted towards them. His tongue dragged down Jack's body and his lips offered kisses to the yearning, supple flesh, and to the child that was growing within his body. The fact that Jack carried Gregory's child only made the desire burn more fiercely within him. The flames were stoked and it was becoming a totally uncontrollable blaze. His breathing was labored and he was filled with this twitching, aching feeling that he *needed* Jack else he was going to lose his mind.

His strong hands manhandled Jack, and the other man offered little resistance. He was willing to let Gregory take him and treat him in any way he wanted, dazed and delirious by the furious passion that raged through the air. A haze burned and the air simmered. Everything pulsed and throbbed inside Gregory. There was a fervent energy that crackled and a blitz that needed to be free. He turned Jack around and pulled him to where he was resting on his knees. He clamped his hands around Jack's hips and then gazed at the sight that awaited him. It felt as though he was intoxicated. He groaned as he pushed his aching erection further towards Jack. It was as though their bodies were magnetized. There was no stopping the union between them. The tight warmth met him and Gregory arched his next back in a paroxysm of pleasure, before all the strength seemed to leave him and he slumped over Jack's back, breathing in all the sweet essence of Jack.

Jack turned around and moaned. Gregory ran his hands all over Jack's body as desire drove them and erotic delight overpowered everything. Their moans harmonized and they found a natural rhythm. Their heartbeats thrummed. Gregory's body was like a jackhammer. Sweat dripped down and sizzled on Jack's skin. Gregory reached forward and ran his hands through Jack's hair. It was slick and clung to his scalp. He tugged Jack's neck back and felt the arch appear in the body, making the pleasure even more tremendous. Then, Gregory reached around and felt Jack's own erection, powerful and taut, slapping against his stomach as Gregory made love to him. Gregory started to play with it, loving the feeling of warm hardness in his hands. As the momentum overwhelmed them Gregory's hand naturally moved back and forward, pleasing and teasing Jack.

Jack's head dropped as he was getting pleasure from two sources. Gregory could feel the strength slipping from him and knew that Jack would have collapsed had he not been held up by Gregory's arousal.

Time had no meaning for them as the world slipped away and left them in this incoherent, chaotic state where the blurriness of the world was just an illusion and all the trauma and pain could be forgotten, burned away by everything that was primal and pure. The moans were a song to Gregory and he focused on them as crackling thunder rippled over him and seized his body like a vice. He felt Jack shudder as warmth flowed out over his hand. Jack's body went limp as everything had been released on him. Feeling this spurred Gregory on for the final deep thrusts and then he too roared in pain as everything burst out of him.

He held his position for a few moments, clutching Jack tightly, letting the vibrant sensations dissipate from his mind. His eyes were closed and sweat dripped down his face. His chest rose and fell as he sank back and collapsed to the mattress. His arm fell across his forehead and all the aching sensations reverberated through his body.

"Well, if this is what you being leader means then I'm all for it," Jack said, exhaling deeply as his body shuddered and tried to recover from the intense session.

Gregory didn't say a thing in reply. He was too exhausted and drained to form any words. The heat was overwhelming and the feelings inside had been uncontrollable. Perhaps being the leader of the wolves had unlocked something inside him, something raw and primal, some previously unknown layer of pleasure that took him to new heights of what was possible. It reminded him of what was most precious to him, of what he was trying to protect.

He was the leader of the wolves, and he would not let anything threaten his people.

Chapter Six

The following morning, Jack's body ached and he was still recovering from the moment after Gregory had returned. It was not as romantic as their previous nights together had been, but the blistering passion wasn't anything that Jack was going to refuse. Even just thinking about it brought a smile to his face and his heart danced. It gave him hope that there was still a lot of happiness to be found amongst the misery, and that just because Lycanthia was in mourning it didn't mean that there wouldn't be a chance for life to flourish.

The king's funeral had given closure to a lot of people, so they were able to return to their regular lives and Lycanthia moved to its usual rhythm. Although people would never forget King Boris there was a practical outlook. As Hank said, 'fish were still waiting to be caught.' It might have seemed heartless to some, but it was testament to the determination of the Lycanthian people to not allow anything to halt their day to day lives.

Of course, as well as the death there was still the matter of the Silvainian threat. As Jack moved around Lycanthia he could feel the silent tension and see the haunted look in people's eyes as they tried to forget about what lay outside the Lycanthian borders. There were more guards on the streets, and people were more suspicious of anyone who didn't look familiar, for they were afraid these people might be Silvainian agents seeking to sow discord or perform another assassination attempt. Jack also noticed how people's eyes drifted naturally to the distant horizon, wondering what was out there waiting to strike.

Gregory had changed ever since the gathering. He was more confident and assured, which in Jack's mind was a welcome change. Still, there seemed to be a great deal that was uncertain for the future, as nobody knew when Silvain was going to make their next move, and unless Lycanthia was going to attack, the initiative was fully with Silvain.

However, for the time being there was a brief respite as the newly crowned Queen had invited Jack and Gregory for a picnic with her and Ferdinand. She was feeling better and wanted something to take her mind off recent events. Gregory was a little nervous as he wasn't sure how to act around Ferdinand.

"Just be nice," Jack said. "If Leah likes him then trust her instincts. If he says anything that seems off then you can tell her about it later. Let's just have a little fun and try to enjoy the time when it's given to us."

Gregory nodded and breathed deeply. Jack worried that he was taking too much on his plate, what with being the Queen's advisor and leader of the wolves, but Gregory accepted it all with a noble demeanor and Jack was proud of him for this.

They met Leah and Ferdinand at the castle, and then walked towards the gardens towards the rear. At this time of day, they were bathed in sunlight and the air was warm. The fragrance of the flowers was light and sweet, and the petals burst with color. Off to the horizon the deep blue of the ocean could be seen, melting into the sapphire brightness of the sky. Jack was a little nervous as he was just a common American while he was dining with two nobles and Gregory, who had a number of impressive titles now, but he hoped that he would be able to fit in.

Ferdinand carried a huge picnic basket that was filled to the brim with a feast prepared by the royal kitchen. Leah had a blanket, which she handed to Gregory so that he might carry it. When they reached their destination, he threw it over the ground and they settled down. Leah curled her legs underneath her body. She still looked pale, and there was a sadness that lined her eyes, but Jack noted how she was trying to make the effort to get on with life despite all she had lost. Ferdinand was certainly handsome, with his eye-catching red hair and lazy smile. He wore a black tunic with gold inlay, and he quickly set about distributing the food, serving Leah first.

Jack's eyes went wide as he saw the feast laid before them. There was an array of sandwiches, baked potatoes, salad, fish, rice, as well as sweetbread, jam, scones, fruit, and a pie. The aroma of the food made Jack's stomach rumble and he helped himself to plenty of food. After all, he was eating for two.

"Well, this is a nice change of pace after the last few days," Ferdinand said, relaxing in the sun. Jack noticed how he found it difficult to keep his eyes off of Leah.

"I quite agree," she said, smiling widely, wiping a crumb away from the corner of her mouth with her little finger.

"So, Ferdinand, are you happy that you have stayed in Lycanthia for a little while?" Gregory asked.

"Definitely, and I much prefer my current accommodation to the dungeons," he said, smiling widely. Leah and Gregory both cringed as he said this, looking away. Ferdinand seemed to be amused by their reaction. He leaned towards Jack and placed a hand by one side of his mouth. "It's always fun to make your hosts squirm when you're an outside," he said in a conspiratorial whisper. Jack couldn't help but laugh.

"I'm sure nothing like that is going to happen again," Gregory said. Ferdinand ran a hand through his hair and nodded in agreement, before turning to Jack.

"So, how did you crazy kids meet? You're American right?" he asked.

Jack nodded. "I am indeed. I was actually on vacation here. My grandfather died and he had some ties to this place. Mom and I came over to see if we could find out a little more about him. Then I met Gregory and, well, I couldn't wait to come back." He glanced towards Gregory and smiled widely, loving the feeling of happiness that swelled within him.

"That's really sweet. Did you find out what you needed to; about your grandfather I mean?" Ferdinand asked.

"I did. I think I know him better now than I might have otherwise," Jack said.

"So, are you planning to go back to America or are you staying here?" Ferdinand asked.

"I'm staying here. There's no way I'm going to leave Gregory, or this place. I mean, just look at it," Jack let his gaze drift along the horizon and took in all the beauty of Lycanthia, from the green grass to the verdant trees, over the glassy ocean, up to the towering stone castle and beyond. "It's breathtaking."

"That it is," Ferdinand said, although his gaze was locked on Leah. She caught the meaning of his words and blushed, giggling softly. Jack smirked and glanced towards Gregory. Oh yes, this Ferdinand was definitely a charmer.

"I have been rather taken with the place myself. My home is…well…it's humble and typical, but I've always felt that it lacks a certain magical quality that Lycanthia has. There's something rare here, something that is hard to find elsewhere. It's the kind of thing where once you see it you can't let yourself let it go," he paused for a moment and let his hair fall across his face. "But perhaps I speak too quickly. After all, I would not wish to pressure the Queen into making a decision before she is ready." He flashed a smile towards Leah.

"I do wish you'd stop calling me Queen. Please, call me Leah, especially here. We're all friends and we don't have to rely on official titles." Leah said with a warm smile. Jack relaxed a little and took the words for himself, even though they had been directed towards Ferdinand. It was strange to think that he was sitting among nobles and a Queen! They were all wearing such fine clothes as well. Ferdinand was wearing a shirt that was the color of midnight with a gold trim running down the sleeves and the middle of the shirt. The top few buttons were open, revealing the hollow of his throat. Leah wore a silver dress that sparkled like the moon on a summer's night. It almost seemed to be alive as it shifted when she moved.

"I think I can live with that," Ferdinand said with a smile. His gaze then turned out towards the horizon and he sighed happily, taking in all the sights that Lycanthia had to offer. It truly was glorious, and whenever Jack took a moment to take his eyes away from Gregory he was stunned by the breathtaking beauty of the horizon. It was idyllic and seemed too pure and good to be attacked. Jack's smile fell from his face as he pictured an army riding over the sloping hills and valleys, leaving charred ground and smoking corpses as they went. It was a grim future and it didn't seem like it should happen, but often in life things never turned out the way they should.

"I know you'd rather we didn't talk about this, but I want to give you my assurance that my father will send an army to help defend Lycanthia if needed," Ferdinand said. His words came like a bolt from the blue and everyone froze. Leah swallowed a lump in her throat and forced a smile.

"That's a very kind offer Ferdinand and I will take it under advisement, but I'd prefer to not talk about that right now. Matters of war take a toll on my mind and as yet we have not heard anything from the Silvainian king. Until there is a formal declaration-" Leah said.

"Do you think he will be honorable enough to offer a formal declaration? From his actions so far, I would not be surprised if he just marches into Lycanthian territory whenever he pleases. He seems to think he can do things on his own terms without consequence. He violates the laws of hospitality and uses cowardly tricks like poison and baits traps. We must assume that he is going to conduct himself in the same manner during a war," Ferdinand said. His tone was a little harsh. It was noble of him to feel so slighted even when the kingdom was not his own, but it was still not the proper place to talk about these things. Jack could tell that Leah was uncomfortable, so he attempted to shift the conversation into another direction.

"I have to admit that I'm still confused why he would even want to attack Lycanthia, especially after all this time. Surely, he has better things to do," Jack said.

"It has to do with an old territorial dispute," Ferdinand said, surprising everyone with the certainty with which he spoke. They looked at him with wide eyes.

"How can you be so certain of King Stewart's motives?" Gregory asked in a terse voice that was filled with suspicion. Ferdinand smirked.

"By studying history. My father ensured that I was well-versed in the kingdoms surrounding us. He thought it was a useful skill to have, because in history there are patterns and if you study it closely enough you can see the weave of choices and consequence winding through time as though it is a tapestry. Back when Lycanthia was first founded Silvain was a prospering kingdom with a bright future. Its mines were producing vast quantities of silver and there seemed no end to the flow of precious metal. The only problem was that their kingdom was located in a harsh land, surrounded by dark jagged mountains and unforgiving terrain. If they were to grow, they needed to expand and find more beautiful land that suited their wealth better and would attract people to live there. But then the founders of Lycanthia settled and seemed to take the land from right under Silvain's nose. I can't imagine they were very happy about that, and it seems as though King Stewart wants to make up for that slight," Ferdinand explained.

"But that's preposterous," Gregory spluttered, "that happened generations ago! Why would they want to retaliate now?"

Ferdinand shrugged. "Perhaps the Silvainians have been planning this for a long time. Perhaps it is just that King Stewart is more ruthless than his ancestors. His motive should not concern us at this moment, only his actions. But it is interesting to study the founding of Lycanthia. The stories surrounding that time are intriguing and speak of a far more magical world than the one we inhabit now. I'm sure you're well aware of the myth that Lycanthia was founded by werewolves?" Ferdinand asked rhetorically. The other three glanced uneasily at each other and all showed signs of unease. Leah wrung her hands. Gregory tugged at his collar. Jack shifted his weight on the picnic blanket. "It's a very interesting story, although it's been dismissed as a strange interpretation. The logical explanation would be that the Lycanthians of old had a symbiotic relationship with the wolves and used them to aid them in battle. It would be safe to assume that word would have spread of this bond and like everything else the story would have grown stranger in the telling."

"Yes, it is an odd story, but one we are proud of," Leah said, breathing with relief. But Ferdinand wasn't finished.

"A story," he said, and grunted a laugh. "I thought it was just a story too before I came here. But then something else happened. While everyone's eyes were on the man who threw the spear, and losing their minds with panic, my eyes were on you Leah. I saw something most surprising. At the moment you were struck you twisted with rage and you became…something else. It was quite remarkable."

"I'm sure you must have been mistaken. It was a harrowing time for us all and I think everyone saw some things they weren't quite sure about," Leah spoke quickly and her face turned away. Jack could almost hear her heart beating. He glanced towards Gregory.

"I'm not a man prone to hallucinations. I know what I saw," Ferdinand said harshly. Leah swallowed a lump in her throat, and Gregory leapt to her defense."

"What is this? What is your plan here? Are you trying to slander us? To blackmail us? What kind of nefarious plot are you working on Ferdinand?" the words shot out of his mouth like bullets.

"I'm not working on any plot," Ferdinand said innocently. "I just wanted to make it clear that I know your secret," his eyes turned towards Leah. "I assumed that you would not tell me freely, so I had to reveal it myself. I do not have any agenda, other than winning your hand. Whoever you choose as your husband must be able to support you and have your trust in all matters, even things like this. I want you to know that you can be assured of my support and confidence. Frankly, I have not been able to get the image out of my mind. It was so…majestic. I am intrigued by all of the possibilities," his eyes gleamed with intrigue, in much the same way that Jack's had when he first learned about Lycanthia. He glanced towards Gregory.

"I think we should go for a walk and leave Ferdinand and Leah to talk," Jack suggested. Gregory was about to protest, but Jack emphasized the idea with a stern look in his eyes.

"Would you mind if we took our leave?" Gregory asked, turning to Leah. The Queen had a stunned look on her face, but she was pleased as well and nodded, tilting her head towards Ferdinand.

"There is much you should know…" she began as Jack and Gregory walked away.

Chapter Seven

"The gall of that man!" Gregory muttered as they walked out of earshot of Ferdinand and Leah. They turned towards the meadow and walked through the green grass. Daisies and dandelions wafted around them as they walked by, and the air had a pleasing aroma. "I can't believe he would just come right out and say it like that. Does he have no idea of respect!"

"Actually, I think he handled the matter well. He didn't want there to be any secrets between them. It's the same thing we went through. I wish that I had been a little braver at the beginning to tell you I knew about what you are," Jack said.

Gregory was softened a little by the reminder of how their love had first bloomed, but it was still difficult to get over the suspicion he had for Ferdinand. He loved Leah like a sister and he didn't want there to be any doubt about the man who courted her.

"I suppose," he muttered, with a scowl on his face.

"Oh come on, don't be like that," Jack nudged him playfully. "It's good that Leah and Ferdinand are getting on so well. She could use some happiness in her life after what she's been through, and he seems like a good sort. I like him."

"You do?"

"Oh yeah, he's forthright, funny, and the man appreciates his history. I think he'd make a good match with Leah. Besides, he's the one who is still standing here despite everything that's happened. That counts for a lot."

"You really think that the Queen's husband should be chosen by default?" Gregory asked skeptically. Jack rolled his eyes.

"No, of course I don't. I think he should be chosen based on the fact that he didn't protest when he was thrown in the dungeon, that he stayed when he was released to still pursue the Queen, that he's actually willing to marry into a kingdom who has had a threat of war against them, and that he's interested in Leah even though he knows she's a werewolf. You and I both know how easy it is for people to feel fear about that rather than be intrigued. The fact that he's still there shows me that Leah means a lot to him, and I wouldn't be so quick to discount him."

Gregory pursed his lips and nodded, sighing. "I suppose you're right. Perhaps I am being too protective of Leah. When you put it like that, I can't imagine anyone else better suited for her, and I'm sure she wouldn't be able to either. I'm also disturbed by the story he told."

"In what way?" Jack asked.

"How can a kingdom hold on to so much hatred for so many generations? It doesn't make sense to me. Surely, they would have been better off focusing on their own ambitions and finding other territory elsewhere? It may not have been the same as this place, but it could still have been better than what they currently have. The fact that they've spent so many years focusing on their anger...it's just astounding that they would waste their time like this."

Jack nodded somberly. "Some people can't get over these perceived slights. I suppose Stewart has vowed to make the past injustices right, but the world has moved on." His voice caught in his throat. "Do you think we can stop him?"

"We have to," Gregory said. He stood proudly and thought of all the wolves at his command. "We will. The wolves are all in agreement that we shall fight if needed alongside the Lycanthian army. If Stewart comes back and wants war, then he shall have it."

Jack smiled and linked his arm in with Gregory's. "It's pretty hot when you speak like that, all commanding and stuff," Jack smiled. Gregory smirked.

"I'm still getting used to the idea. I still can't believe I'm the leader of the pack."

"I can. I can't think of anyone better. You're a good man Gregory and I know that you're going to lead the pack well."

"Are you sure you're okay with me doing this? I know that it just puts me in danger, and the last thing I want to do is put myself in danger when we have a life growing inside you."

"At first, I was a little unsure and I suppose my first reaction was wishing we could just push this all away and escape the threat, but that quickly faded. I know you're proud to be a wolf, and I'm proud for you. Part of that means being in the pack, and leading the pack is such a great honor I would never ask you to turn it down. By defending the pack, you are defending our child and I know that love can also be a powerful ally. I would hope it would inspire you to fight that little bit longer and little bit harder."

"I'm sure it will. I won't let anyone keep me from you. I don't care how much they feel slighted by ancient deals," Gregory said. He leaned over and kissed Jack on his forehead. They stopped for a moment and enjoyed a more intimate embrace, eventually lowering themselves down onto the soft meadow, surrounding themselves with the sweet scent of flowers and warm embrace of their love.

They ended up falling into each other's arms and enjoyed being alone. It was funny how the double date had ended up with the two couples splitting off. Now that Gregory had more of a chance to think about it he was pleased for Leah as Ferdinand did seem a fine choice, and of course Gregory would always be there to watch closely over him in case he ever made a mistake. If he ever dared hurt Leah, he would tear Ferdinand limb from limb.

Despite all the sorrow that had drenched Lycanthia in recent times, there was still much happiness to be found. He and Jack were expecting a baby, Leah and Ferdinand seemed to be getting on well, and Emily and Hank's romance was blossoming as well. Even in the most despairing times happiness could be found, and this was something that Gregory tried to remind himself, even when the prospect of war was like a drumbeat in the back of his mind. At one point there must have been a shadow pass across his eyes as Jack turned to him and asked him if he was okay.

"I'm fine," Gregory said, forcing a smile. Jack seemed unconvinced though.

"You know, we haven't really spoken about it…about what happened in Maugrim's Pass. It was very brave of you to go there. I'm proud of you for what you did," Jack said.

Gregory grunted. "What did I do? I ran away and left my King to die."

"At his request. If you had stayed you would have died too and Leah would never have been saved. Things would have been even worse now." His voice caught on his emotion. "Our child would have grown up never knowing you."

Gregory turned towards Jack. His face was like stone, and his heart was heavy as it always was when he thought about that terrible moment, of the arrows hurtling through the air, of Boris' frantic expression, bellowing at him to turn and run, of having to look at all the lifeless expressions on Lycanthian faces with the whisper of death all around him. He closed his eyes, but then felt a caress on the side of his face.

"Hey, hey," Jack said gently. "It's okay. That didn't happen. Our child *is* going to know you. We're going to become a family."

"That's true for now, but what about next time? What if I don't come back?" Gregory asked. Jack pursed his lips and moved his hand down to Gregory's chest.

"Then we'll have to deal with that, but I'm not going to define my life by what might happen. I'm proud of you for defending your people's honor and nothing is going to change that. I know that it's hard and I wish you never had to go through it. I hope you know that you can always talk to me about it and I'm always here for you," Jack said.

Gregory nodded in understanding and nestled his head against Jack's, breathing in the smell of the man he loved. His hand moved over Jack's stomach, sensing the glow of life that grew inside him.

"No matter what happens I'm going to make sure this child gets the best life it possibly can. I don't want it to miss out on anything."

"He or she is going to be so lucky," Jack smiled. "I was thinking as well, I hope you don't mind, but if it's a boy I'd like to name him after my grandfather."

Gregory smiled. "That's okay because I was thinking if it's a girl, I'd like to name her after my mother."

It was an easy agreement to make. "I know this is going to make our parents happy."

"Yes," Gregory said. "Speaking of our parents, don't you think it's a little strange that if things end up going as well for them as they have for us that we might end up stepbrothers?"

Jack squirmed a little. "It has, and I've tried my best to not think about it. I suppose it's just something we're going to have to live with for the sake of their happiness," he said. Gregory smiled and nodded, and sighed. He gazed up at the sky and lost himself in the wispy clouds and the eternal blue that seemed to go on forever.

"When I used to think about the future it was always in an abstract sense. There was a feeling that it would never actually come for me, at least not in the way I wanted it to. I never thought I'd actually fall in love or have a family. I assumed that I would always be the kind of person who wanted things, but never got to have them."

"I suppose it goes to show that you can never tell what's going to happen in the future," Jack said. Gregory nodded.

"I'm glad things didn't work out that way though. Even now the future seems so strange. I don't know what to hope for or what to expect. In some ways I don't want to expect anything. This child is going to surprise us both and I almost don't want to think about the person he or she is going to grow up to be, because I know that no matter what I think of they're going to be different than the image I have in my mind."

"I know. He or she is going to have the best of both of us though, and all the love in the world. And then we'll see what happens. I know it's romantic to think that things are written in the stars and that destiny plays a part in our lives. It's sweet to think that there was something pulling us together even though we lived in two different worlds, but I prefer to believe in a world where it was chance that we met, but we found something in each other and held on tightly to that. I think it's more romantic to think about a world where we made the most of our opportunity and decided to choose each other, even though we knew the odds were against us."

"I like that outlook as well. Can I ask you a question; if you hadn't found out you were pregnant, would you still have come back to Lycanthia?"

Jack nodded without hesitation. "I was already planning the return trip as soon as I left. The main thing I struggled with was Mom. I hated the thought of leaving her alone. I knew that I had to live my own life, but every time I thought of her sitting alone in the house without anyone to talk to or love, it just broke my heart. I didn't know if it was going to be harder to come over here and live with guilt at leaving her, or stay in America and live with regret at never seeing you again. Thankfully, I never had to make that choice and Mom has managed to open her mind. It all turned out for the best really."

"I was thinking about coming to see you as well. I hated that I couldn't leave because of what happened with Leah. But it always felt as though we had unfinished business. I hated that I didn't tell you the truth about myself. It burned in my heart, and I'm glad that I was able to share that with you eventually."

"Me too."

"You know though, I was talking with father and even though we might not be making plans for the child he is. He's already decided that he's going to take our child out on the boat with him and try and train them as a fisherman."

"That doesn't surprise me," Jack chuckled. "I don't mind that either. Hank is a good man. He's the kind of father that I always wanted to have. You just look at him and know that you can trust him."

Gregory smiled, because that's exactly the way he thought about his father.

"You've never really spoken about your father. What happened?" Gregory asked. Whenever the conversation had ever drifted towards the subject of Jack's father, Jack had always grown quiet. Everyone had their secrets, and Gregory hadn't pushed to find out the truth. He had always assumed that Jack would tell him when he was ready, but there were occasions when he wanted to nudge him along with a gentle question. It seemed that on this occasion Jack was more willing to talk about his past.

"He…was not a good man. I used to think he was, of course, when I was younger and could only see the world he wanted me to see. I never understood why Mom was so unhappy, why she was crying all the time. Dad used to take me out to play ball and to football games and things, but there were other times when he wasn't there, like at school plays. Mom always told me that he was called into work or something had come up. When I was older, I found out that it was just because he didn't care about things like that. He only took me to things that he liked doing. He couldn't see past himself or his own interests. I grew up and to be honest I wasn't even interested in baseball or football or car races, but I kept going because it was the only time I got to spend with him. I wish I had said something else because I could see how unhappy Mom was, but I figured that's what all marriages were like behind closed doors. And then one day I came home from school and Mom was crying. She was actually trembling, and to this day I don't know if it was more from anger or sadness. She sat me down and she told me that Dad had left and he wasn't coming back.

"I remember feeling so…hollow. I couldn't actually believe what she was talking about. I didn't understand why. Was something wrong? Was he ill? She shook her head and she told me that she'd been debating all day what to actually tell me, whether to try and cloak things in a way that I could understand, or just to tell me the truth. In the end she decided that I was old enough to handle the truth and that I deserved to know the kind of man my father was. She told me about all the drinking and how he'd do whatever he wanted when he wanted, how he expected her to stay at home and basically be a maid for him. This is when she told me about how he never was working when I was doing something important, he just didn't want to come. She told me how he had cheated on her in the past, but she had forgiven him for the sake of the family and the marriage. She told me that over the years she had lost herself. Then she told me how Dad had just left because he'd found someone else he wanted to be with, and that was that. He hadn't even left me a note or anything, as though he didn't care at all. I just...I didn't know what to think. I knew he wasn't the perfect Dad or anything like that, but I never thought he'd just up and leave without saying goodbye."

"What happened then?" Gregory asked softly, reaching out to show Jack some compassion.

"Grandpa came over. I went to my room. I could still hear them talking through the walls though. Grandpa was furious and declared that he was going to do everything he could to get back at Dad, but Mom calmed him down. Given everything I know now, I imagine Grandpa must have been wishing he were still a werewolf," Jack offered a wry smile. "Grandpa took me out and I stayed with him for a few days while Mom got rid of all Dad's stuff. Grandpa made sure to tell me that this wasn't about me, it was all about him, and that any mistake was all his. It was hard not to believe that it was about me though. Surely there was something wrong with me for him to not even bother to say goodbye?"

Gregory knew the question was rhetorical, but even so he hugged Jack tightly and made sure to remind Jack that he loved him and that there was nothing wrong with him at all. Jack wiped a tear from his eye as he continued.

"Anyway, I had a long talk with Mom. She said if I wanted to, I could try and have a relationship with Dad, even though he had made it quite clear he didn't want one. I thought about it for a long time. Even though I knew things weren't the way they seemed I still thought fondly of the time we'd spent together as kids. I also wanted to know just what he actually thought of me and how he could leave me without saying anything. Grandpa took me aside and he told me that I was unlikely to get a satisfactory answer, and that sometimes in life we never got the luxury of closure. Sometimes we just had to keep going and leave the pain behind.

"I decided if Dad wanted to seek me out and speak to me, he could, but I wasn't going to go running after him like some puppy. I still had Mom and Grandpa, and I knew they loved me, so I focused on that. I tried as hard as I could to forget about Dad and cherish the family that actually wanted me."

"I'm so sorry that had to happen and you had to go through that," Gregory said.

"Me too. I did ask Mom if there was ever actually any point when Dad wanted me, and she said that when they found out she was pregnant he was scared and nervous, but he didn't walk away. He said he wanted to do right by her. And then the more time that went by the more he just seemed to put up with things. I don't remember them, obviously, but apparently there were times when I would cry and instead of trying to calm me down, he just got annoyed with me and hit the wall, saying things like I wasn't what he expected. Mom tried to reassure me by saying that some people just aren't meant to be a parent. I guess that's right. I think deep down I've always been afraid that maybe I'll turn out like him."

As soon as those words slipped out of Jack's mouth, Gregory cupped Jack's head in his hands and pressed his forehead against Jack's. Their faces were so close that their breath swirled together and their lips brushed against each when Gregory spoke.

"You're nothing like him. I know you'd do anything for our child. You don't have to define yourself by him," he said. Jack smiled and kissed Gregory tenderly.

"I know, it's just an irrational fear that I have to deal with. I've been thinking a lot about what kind of parent I'm going to be. I know nobody can know for certain, but I've learned from my father what *not* to do."

"To be honest I think that as long as we're patient and kind and make every decision out of love that's all we have to do," Gregory said. "Maybe that's making it sound a little too simple," he added with a laugh. Jack nodded and let out a long breath, as though he released a lot of tension that had remained within his heart. "Did you ever actually see your Dad again?"

Jack arched his eyebrows and wrung his hands together. "Yeah, although it was just a matter of chance rather than me seeking him out. I was at the mall and I saw him through a crowd. Our eyes locked. I knew instantly that he was him, even though his hair was greyer and he looked as though he had put on a little more weight. Time seemed to freeze as we stared at each other. I was tempted to charge through the crowd and yell at him, make a complete scene and shame him for leaving me without ever saying goodbye. But I just didn't have it in me. I realized then that whatever damage he had done, I just didn't care. If I meant nothing to him then why should he mean anything to me? I saw him coming towards me, but I knew then that nothing he said would make a difference. The best thing he could have done was apologize, even though the chances of that were slim. But even then, what good would an apology have done? I walked away and disappeared into the crowd, leaving him behind."

"I think you made the right decision. I can't imagine he had anything worth saying."

"So yeah...that's my story," Jack said, offering a weak smile. Gregory held him tightly and whispered in his ear, telling him that he never had to feel alone again, and that he was surrounded by people who loved him. Jack smiled and when Gregory looked into his eyes, he did see the future, and it shone brightly. The anguish in his own heart melted away whenever he was with Jack, and it was just as pure a release as it was when he became a wolf.

"There is one other matter we need to talk about though," Gregory said. "And that's what to do about our two lives. I know that you're American and if you wanted our child to be raised in America I-"

Jack stopped him by pressing a finger against his lips.

"I don't have any feelings towards America Gregory. Everything I care about is here. This is where I belong. This is home to me now. There's no other place I would rather be, and I want our child to know their birthright. My future is in Lycanthia." He turned and looked out towards the horizon. "How could anyone ever think about leaving this place?"

Chapter Eight

Nine months later

The months had passed without incident, which was pleasing for everyone in Lycanthia. The tension and fear of a Silvainian invasion had been tempered somewhat, although Leah and Gregory were still making preparations for when the enemy did attack. They couldn't believe that King Stewart would stop his assault after his initial gambit to kill the queen had failed. Such hatred that inspired an act like that would not be quelled easily. But the people of Lycanthia were not going to let themselves be defined by fear, nor were they going to let it stop them from living their lives. Life continued as normal as it could. Gregory grew into his role as leader of the wolf pack, and Jack...well, Jack just grew. His belly swelled with life and he suffered all the regular ailments of pregnancy. His mother and Leah were there to help him through it, as were Tristan and Shane, who had been through the same thing themselves.

Jack was given a room in the castle where he could live without fear of his secret being let out. The idea of a man becoming pregnant would surely take the world by storm if it ever slipped out, and Jack didn't want to be the focus of media attention. Instead, he stayed in the castle and wore wide and baggy clothes whenever he had to walk elsewhere. Meanwhile, Leah and Ferdinand's relationship had deepened. It was rare to see the Queen go anywhere without Ferdinand by her side. It seemed as though the Queen had been able to confide in him about all her secrets, and when Jack saw her, he saw her glow with the same kind of love that he had for Gregory. And, thankfully, he saw the same thing radiating from his mother and Hank too. With Jack and Gregory spending most of their time in the castle, Hank and Emily had enjoyed their privacy together. Both of them had scars from previous relationships, but in each other they had found a way to heal their wounds and find some happiness. It was such a joy for Jack to see his mother happy after spending so many years with her clutching a stone of sorrow.

Lycanthia was abuzz with the announcement of a royal wedding. It was going to be a small ceremony as Leah didn't want to welcome any strangers who might be agents of Silvain, but it was going to be a triumphant occasion and Gregory was going to have the honor of standing beside the Queen as she made her vows.

But Jack had something else on his mind. The days of his pregnancy grew shorter. Tristan and Shane had tried to prepare him as best they could, but the closer the due date came, the more Jack became worried something was going to go wrong. After all, men weren't supposed to have children and he worried deeply that something bad was going to happen. It had been nine months since the last tragedy, so it seemed they were due one. Gregory tried to reassure him nothing like that was the case, but nothing could sweep the fears away from Jack's heart.

Now, all he wanted was for the child to be born. He was overjoyed when he felt the baby move inside him. It was such a profound thing to feel a life developing inside his body. It was more intimate than anything else, and although he loved Jack with all his heart, he knew he wasn't going to love anything as much as he loved this child. It was completely and irrevocably unconditional love in the purest sense of the word.

Tristan and Shane had given him other words of warning as well.

"Being the human father of a wolf is never an easy task. The wolf side is so primal and deep in the blood that the human part can be lost. I had a lot of arguments with Boris, who often said that he wanted to get rid of his human half completely and be a wolf all the time," Shane said.

"Even with Leah it was difficult. I'm actually surprised she's made the transition so well. It's important to not take it personally. It's going to be difficult because Gregory and your child are going to share something that is such a deep bond, and we can never have anything like that, but it doesn't mean they're going to love you any less," Tristan reassured. Jack nodded and tried to take it all in. There was so much he didn't understand, so much that he knew he was going to have to cope with and he was unsure if he was prepared, but deep down h knew that as long as he loved this child it was all going to be okay.

As the preparations for the royal wedding were being made, Jack went into labor.

✳✳✳

The pain was like nothing he had ever known before. It lanced through the middle of his body and radiated out, making every muscle ache deeply. His body arched. Sweat dripped down his face. Gregory was by his side, clutching his hand. Pain relief had been given to Jack, although it didn't seem to make much of a difference. A sheet had been raised above his chest and his stomach had been numbed so that he couldn't see the incision being made into his flesh, or the baby being lifted from his stomach. It was still a miracle that this had even happened and he had his grandfather to thank. Something deep in his blood, ancient and sacred, had made this all possible. Adrenaline sang within him and a delirious feeling took hold as the body tried to do all it could to deflect the pain. Jack clamped his eyes shut as he heard vague voices around him, and felt Gregory's presence beside him. Jack whispered a hope that everything would be alright and that the baby would be healthy and safe.

Then, through all the blissful pain and the aching, sharp spasms in his body, he heard a piercing scream that drove everything away. It was the anguished scream of new life, of healthy lungs, of his child.

Jack opened his eyes. At first, he wasn't sure whether tears or sweat blurred his vision. He opened his arms as he felt the weight of his newborn son. So small, so fragile, so beautiful. Jack and Gregory leaned over their baby and commented on the inherited features and the beauty, and they shared in their love for each other. They kissed deeply and then gently caressed their son's body.

"Welcome to the world Michael," Jack said, and he beamed with hope and love and everything that was good.

∗∗∗

As it happened, nothing had gone wrong with the birth at all and all Jack needed was some time to recover before he was back at full health. He did make a remark that he was never doing that again though. They were given some time to rest in their castle chamber and then the visitors started to pour in. First came Emily and Hank, proud grandparents, basking in the glow of the new life. Then came the Queen, welcome, the new subject into the Lycanthia. She beamed with pride, especially as she was going to be the boy's godmother. Shane, Tristan, and Triss were there too. It didn't make up for the loss they had suffered. Nothing could, but a new life was always something to rejoice about and it made them all think about the future. Jack caught Leah and Ferdinand looking with meaning at each other, and he wondered if perhaps another announcement would soon follow the royal wedding.

But when all the visitors had left, Jack and Gregory were alone with their child. Jack was filled with complete wonder and awe at the sight of the baby. The wriggling body was beautiful, the smile was magical, and the wide, sparkling eyes were so filled with love and wonder it was as though all the possibilities of the world flowed out before them like a glittering rainbow. They tickled Michael's belly and they melted when he clutched their finger with his tiny hands. He was alive, and he was only in the world because of their love. Of all the magic that existed in Lycanthia this was the most precious.

"He's so beautiful. I can't get over how much I love him. It feels as though my heart is going to burst," Gregory said. Jack knew exactly how he felt. They kissed deeply and then cuddled in the bed together with their son, a happy family.

***

About a week passed and Jack had recovered well. The baby was healthy and they returned to live with Emily and Hank for a while to give the grandparents a chance to dote on their new grandchild, although eventually they would move into the castle permanently as that was where Gregory had to be in his position as royal advisor. The sorrow that had plagued Lycanthia was in the past and the days were looking a little brighter. It was days before the wedding was taking place, and everyone was preparing their finest gowns and tunics to wear on this most auspicious of occasions. Even Michael was going to be cloaked in splendor. Hank and Emily had agreed that after the ceremony they would watch over Michael for the night so that Gregory and Jack could properly enjoy themselves, as they had been through a lot and needed some time to themselves.

The group went to the castle for the wedding. There were just as many people attending the wedding as there had been King Boris' funeral, but the mood was entirely different. There was a delegation of Ferdinand's family as well. His father seemed to be in a good mood and proud that his son was getting married. Jack settled in a seat with Michael resting on his lap as he waited for proceedings to unfold. Gregory rushed off to be by Leah's side. Ferdinand waited anxiously at the dais, and then rich music filled the courtyard as Leah walked down the aisle. Tristan had his arm linked in with hers, eyes glistening with tears. Gregory walked behind her. The bride looked breathtaking. She wore a sparkling silver gown. It was as though the moon had fallen from the sky and draped itself around her, having pulled stars in her orbit as well. These settled on her like stardust and made her twinkle. Gregory had informed Jack that the gown was one her great-grandmother had worn. Freya had been a proud and fierce Queen, and had reigned through a tumultuous time. It is said that Leah was the spitting image of the wise Queen, who had sadly departed the world before Jack or Gregory had had a chance to meet her. but her name was always uttered with respect, and her legacy continued through her blood.

Leah took her position beside Ferdinand, who beamed with pride. Vows were exchanged, as were rings, and the crowd was quiet with reverence as they witnessed this most noble and hallowed of rituals. Jack was glad that Leah had found some happiness. It was one thing to marry a suitor for an alliance or political gain, but quite another to marry for love and after all she had been through, she definitely deserved that. He knew she had lost something precious after being cured of the poison, but at least she had embraced life and accepted that she could still be happy. Jacks grandfather had shown that there was still a life waiting for wolves after they lost their ability to shift, and he was glad that she had discovered the same thing.

It would lead to a change in the way Lycanthian society worked though. Before, there had always been a wolf on the throne. It was yet to see if Leah's children would display the characteristics of a wolf, or if the throne and the wolf pack would have to be kept separate. However, given what had happened with Jack it seemed as though wolf blood was strong and the magic lingered even when the ability to shift into a wolf was taken away. If he could give birth to Michael then he wouldn't be surprised if Leah could give birth to a little baby wolf of her own.

Once the married couple was presented to the people of Lycanthia there was a huge cheer and applause erupted. Jack shifted Michael around in his arms so he could applause to. He pointed up towards Gregory, although of course Michael didn't understand what was happening. There was a great feast held outside where everyone could eat heartily and fill their bellies. Music played and people danced. Wine and beer flowed freely. Hank was particularly proud that he had caught a huge haul of fish for the wedding.

Everyone was in good spirits and it seemed as though life could not get any better than this. The moon hung in the sky, a pale sphere that blessed the union and all of Lycanthia. The fire of torches burned and crackled, illuminating the courtyard. Gregory came back as soon as he was able and embraced his family.

Leah and Ferdinand were swarmed with people who wanted to congratulate them, so Gregory and Jack kept their distance and instead spoke with Triss and Shane, who were pleased to see such love and happiness bloom. There was of course mention of Boris. Everyone wished that the king had been there to see his daughter wed, and they cursed the king of Silvain from preventing that from happening.

Jack couldn't help but notice the guards that were stationed in the shadows, watching things like a hawk. Gregory had made sure they were prepared in case anything should happen. With all the preparations it had been impossible to keep the wedding a secret, so they hadn't even tried. Gregory was afraid that it would be the target of an attack as the entire kingdom would be preoccupied with the wedding so it was an opportune time to strike, but so far it had developed without any trouble. Jack was beginning to wonder if the threat from the Silvainian king had been empty after all, and if the attack had ended with King Boris' death.

He tried to put those kinds of thoughts out of his mind considering that there were far happier things to think about. He was glad to see Emily beaming with happiness and love. Everything had turned out for the best and it was all because they had come to this magical place. For Jack it had all started with his grandfather's stories and a hint that there was some truth to them. It had led Jack to this, to falling in love and having a child of his own and being surrounded with so much happiness his heart almost burst.

He handed Michael to Hank and then grabbed Gregory's arm, dragging him away from a conversation with Triss into the middle of the dance floor where he started to dance, throwing himself into his happiness and the delirium of the night.

***

By the time the crowd started to disperse Gregory and Jack had gotten drunk and then sobered up again. Their muscles ached from dancing so much and their sides hurt from laughing. Eventually they had spent more time with the married couple, who were relaxed and bright with their love. It did come time for the night to draw to an end. Leah and Ferdinand cast subtle glances at each other and it was clear they only wanted to fulfill their obligations before they could slip away and enjoy the delights that were kept for people in love. As soon as they were able, they slipped away, giggling, sharing the secrets lovers shared.

"I think it's time for us to be getting to bed," Jack said. "I'm fully recovered from giving birth by the way," he hinted. A smile widened over Gregory's face. He clamped his hand around Jack's and strode away, not wanting to waste another minute. Most of the people they knew had already left. Emily and Hank had taken Michael away to put him to bed. Jack felt strange whenever he was apart from Michael, but he knew it was healthy to have some distance between them, and there were some things that couldn't be done while in the presence of their child. The people of Lycanthia would stay in the courtyard and enjoy all the hospitality offered long into the next morning, but

91

for Jack and Gregory it was time to embrace the shadows and the comfort of a warm bed.

They threw themselves into their room and smiled at each other as they wrapped their hands around each other's bodies. They explored each other's hair and back and tugged at the clothes, wanting to strip away the layers of modesty to reveal nothing but flesh and lust underneath. Jack laughed as he was pushed to the bed and sank in the billowing softness of the pillows and satin sheets. His breath was silenced as he caught Gregory's lips in his own, and they shared a deep kiss. Their bodies came together, entwining like vines. Their hands met and their fingers twisted together before breaking apart and sliding over exposed flesh. Hearts beat furiously and frantically, finding the same rhythm. Sweat prickled on skin. Smiles turned into kisses and kisses turned into fervent moans.

Their bodies twitched with arousal and surging blood sang as it careened underneath their skin. A tsunami flooded through them and lightning crackled wherever they touched, leaving vibrant tingles that pulsed and throbbed. Their hands reached down to dark, shadowy places. Making love had been much different while Jack had been pregnant. His body had been unwieldy and various parts of him had been so sensitive he hadn't been able to lose himself fully into the abyss of pleasure, so now he had much to make up for. He breathed in Gregory's musky scent and pressed his hands against the supple flesh. He buried himself in the nook of Gregory's neck and closed his eyes, becoming intoxicated with the essence of the man he loved. His hand curled around the back of Gregory's neck and played with his hair. Gregory murmured in response and replied with gentle caresses of his own, caresses in the sweet spots that only he knew, because he was a master of Jack's body in a way that nobody else had ever been before, not even Jack himself.

Their instincts called each other and Jack found himself being driven by instinct. He slid down Gregory's body, dragging his lips and tongue with him. Kisses were planted down the middle of Gregory's body and they were precipitated by his hands, which found the hot warmth in between Gregory's thighs. Jack reached down and stroked the inside of his thighs at first, before he moved his hand up and ran his palm along the long, thick shaft. He moaned as he curled his fingers around Gregory's erection and started to play with it, stroking it gently, squeezing it to feel Gregory twitch. He ran his thumb over the mushroom tip and then pressed his lips in a kiss against the thatch of hair that rested around the base, before he opened his mouth wide and took Gregory's organ inside. Warm saliva dripped down, coating the shaft, drizzling like honeyed glaze over a thick chunk of meat. Jack tasted the sex and gorged himself on the sensation. His moans were stifled as he felt the heat on his tongue, pressing against the back of his throat.

"I want you too," Gregory moaned in a strained whisper. He pawed at Jack's body. Jack adjusted himself, shifting his body around so that he ran parallel against Gregory, pressing himself against him. He never took his mouth off Gregory's cock, not for an instant. Then a whole new pleasure came swarming through him, striking like lightning. He gaped for a moment, losing his sucking rhythm, before resuming, getting used to the way Gregory's tongue lashed around his cock, swirling like a maelstrom. The two men wrapped their arms around each other's legs, gripping on tightly, locking themselves in this cycle of pleasure and bliss and harmony. Their raw love blossomed in this intense miasma of heat, making the air shimmer around them. Sweat hissed and sizzled as it trickled down flesh. Jack could feel the tension rising within them, simmering and swirling like a beast underneath the surface of the ocean, waiting to strike with fury. He groaned as he pulled himself away.

"I need to be closer to you," Jack whispered. Gregory looked groggy and desire was smeared over his lips. They rocked on their knees and came together, kissing each other as wildly as they had done that first time they had let their attraction free, on the beach after searching for treasure. They had found something even more precious than gold that day. Their lips crashed against each other in a blaze of ecstasy and then Jack pushed Gregory down. He then straddled Gregory, lowering himself slowly on Gregory's manhood, feeling the sweet tightness inside him. His mouth widened into a large 'O' as the pleasure rippled all over his face and across his body. He leaned forward, wincing as pain blurred with sweet, sweet pleasure. His hands landed on Gregory's strong chest. Gregory's face twisted with tension. His hands reached around Jack's waist and helped to guide the rocking, swaying movements as Jack used his body to make the pleasure flare between them.

He angled himself so that he could see the point where their bodies met. His own erection stood tall. Gregory moved one of his hands around to play with him, using the natural momentum to call the pleasure to him. Blood and lust swirled around Jack's mind as he lost all sense and coherent thought. He could feel his strength buckling and he gave himself wholly to the sensations that whirled through him. They were primal and raw, yet profound and deep. It was as though his heart cracked open and all the love and lust poured out, coating him and Gregory in its slick warmth.

Moans crashed around his mind and bellowed in the air. Gregory's grip tightened on his body and pleasure burst forth. Jack was unable to hold onto everything as he gave it all to Gregory, watching it spurt out in a hot frothing jet that spread all over Gregory's chest and stomach. Feeling the heat rain over him was the last thing Gregory needed to drive himself to the vibrant release. His body shuddered and with a few final thrusts he drove himself into Jack's body, erupting a warm wave into Jack.

The two men collapsed after it was over, smiling at each other, dazed and delirious. Jack groaned as he closed his eyes and breathed in the scents of their sex and love. It was all magical. It was all because he was here, in Lycanthia, with the man he loved, and he didn't want to be anywhere else.

Chapter Nine

It had been a strange time for Gregory. While Jack had been preparing for the birth, Gregory had felt largely out of sorts. He could be there for support, of course, but it was Jack's body that was experiencing this wondrous thing. He couldn't help but feel a moment of jealousy at the fact that Jack had this natural bond with their child, but that was tempered by the knowledge that the child would be a wolf. Both parents would share something with the child that the other could not. Then came the birth and as soon as Gregory saw Michael for the first time he fell in love, completely and utterly, and his entire world changed. It was the deepest, most powerful feeling he had ever known and there wasn't anything he wouldn't have done to protect the child. Suddenly he understood his own father better as well, and a new perspective came to him.

He wondered how long it would take him to get used to being a father, but it didn't take him long at all. He soon got used to the idea and the actions of being a father came naturally to him. When he presented the new wolf child to the pack, they all howled in recognition and acceptance. Gregory looked forward to the day when he could teach Michael all about being a wolf and what it meant to have this supernatural blood flowing through his veins. It struck him that if things had gone differently in the past and Jack's grandfather hadn't rid himself of his wolf side, Jack might well have been a werewolf too. Still, it didn't matter that he wasn't. Gregory loved Jack for exactly who he was.

Gregory was honored to be at Leah's side for the wedding, although he found that he couldn't enjoy the day as much as other people. Suspicion and paranoia lurked in his mind. Although it had been a long time since they had heard word from Silvain, Gregory wasn't about to lose sight of the threat. A wedding seemed the ideal place to strike, so he insisted that guards be placed all around the castle in case an enemy agent managed to sneak in. Leah wasn't particularly happy about this as she didn't want her wedding to become a battlefield, but they ended up compromising; she allowed Gregory to station guards around the courtyard in the shadows, where they were out of sight and wouldn't remind people of the danger that lurked elsewhere in the world.

Even though the wedding happened without being interrupted he still couldn't shake the feeling that *something* was coming for Lycanthia. After he and Jack had made love and Jack was sleeping, Gregory walked to the window and looked out upon the night. King Stewart was likely out there, plotting Lycanthia's downfall, and as leader of the wolves Gregory was one of the men standing between him and his great plot.

The following days were all happy. Gregory had confided his worries with Jack, although only once as Gregory didn't want to mar these happy days with his anxieties, for it was right that they should be filled with happiness without being defined by sorrow. But still this shadow lurked within Gregory's heart and then, a few days after the wedding, the mood in Lycanthia changed by one small delivery.

Even though the wedding ceremony had been confined to those in Lycanthia, many neighboring kingdoms sent gifts to honor the marriage. These flowed in day after day, and much of Leah and Ferdinand's time was spent opening these gifts. But then they received a small package that did not come with a note. Leah furrowed her brow as she opened it, and then her face turned ashen white. Her hands trembled as she looked in the box. Everyone wondered what could have been inside to elicit such a reaction, and a dark worry swelled in the pit of Gregory's stomach, as though a stone weighed him down.

Hushed whispers were rampant through the royal court as they all waited with anticipation to see what this gift was. Some mistook Leah's reaction for one of surprise and excitement, but Gregory was close enough to hear the fear in her heart. She reached in and pulled out a tattered fragment of clothing, the same clothing that Boris had worn on that fateful day when they had met in Maugrim's Pass. Along with this was a lock of hair, still as fresh as when Gregory had last seen him.

"What is this?" Leah's words were harsh. "What are they trying to say? Are they trying to tell me he's alive?" Her eyes shot to Gregory. The color drained from his face. He thought back to that day.

"N-No. It's...he died. He..." his words faltered as he remembered the scene or enemies bearing down on Boris, then he had fled and ran away. "I...I could see no way out for him."

"It seems as though they have spared his life," Leah said sharply.

"But why now? Why after all this time are they sending this to you?" Gregory asked.

"I don't know. But I'm going to find out. Summon the forces. Summon everything you have! I am going to meet this Silvainian King myself." She crumpled the cloth in her hand as her fist closed around it. Gregory began to protest. As advisor he had to make sure she understood the dangers, but Leah was like her father when she had made her mind up about something. She wasn't going to be kept from this fight.

***

The news soon spread about the gift that had been given, and people wondered if Boris was truly alive or if this was some other trick by King Stewart. Gregory was inclined to believe the latter, and he was determined to prepare for the worst. This time he wasn't going to be caught in the same situation as before, nor was he going to let King Stewart have the upper hand. He and Leah had already agreed they were going to use everything at Lycanthia's disposal, and that meant driving forward with a force of men and werewolves.

Gregory told them this plan at the Gathering, but some offered concerns.

"I want to defend Lycanthia and King Boris' name, but we've kept our secret for so long. What if this is all a plan to get us out in the light?" one man asked, understandably worried about what might happen after the battle.

"Damn our secret. It's always been a noose around our neck. It's time to announce ourselves to the world. I hate going about my business keeping my secret from my friends and colleagues. If anyone wants to judge us for being wolves then they can live somewhere else. I'd prefer to be out in the open. Most people know anyway, or they at least suspect something from all the stories," another said. The debate raged for a while and there were moments when Gregory worried that he was going to lose control of the gathering, but then he remembered that he was the leader and he should stamp his authority on proceedings.

"The wolves have always been linked with Lycanthia and we are not going to shirk our duty now. This is not up for debate. We are going into battle. If any of you are worried about revealing your secret then you do not have to run with us. The world is a different place than it has been before. King Stewart is no doubt expecting us to be hidden and secret, but we must trust in those around us otherwise things will never change for the better. We must open ourselves up rather than hiding what is so wonderful about us. The people who really matter will accept us for who we are," he said, thinking about his own experience and knowing how wonderful it was to be accepted by Jack.

The wolves around him seemed to accept this line of reasoning. It took some longer than others to come around fully, but he had their backing and they agreed to run alongside the human forces. Some were actually eager for a fight as there hadn't been a war in their lifetimes, and they were looking forward to getting revenge on King Stewart. Gregory was pleased to have the strength of the wolves behind him, but he was still wary as King Stewart was a wily man and it was likely he had some trick.

***

A small force was left in Lycanthia, along with all the general civilians, including Jack and Michael. Gregory hated leaving them like this but he promised he would return. He kissed Jack hard, and gave Michael a long hug before he left. A tear flowed down his cheek, but he was determined to return and to live out the rest of his life, to see his son grow up. Hank went to war with him, and Leah and Ferdinand also rode out towards Silvain. The air was alive with the thunder of hooves and the howl of wolves. The pack of wolves were a stream as they sprinted over the hills, a great pack moving with a single mind. The Lycanthian army rode towards the foreboding kingdom of Silvain, characterized by its jagged mountains and its cold air. The trembling of the earth caused by the might army must have alerted King Stewart to their presence as he was waiting with an army as they arrived. There was a great cage behind him, with metal doors that were solid and thick, but Gregory could not see what was held inside. Casper stood by his father's side, wearing his sneer. Ferdinand curled his lip and pointed his lance, while Leah remained regal on her horse.

"I see you got my message," Stewart said. "And I'm so glad you brought your friends. It's exactly what I wanted. I hope they're all here. This is the last time they're going to see the light of day."

"You speak too rashly. What is the meaning of this message?" Leah demanded. Stewart's lips curled into a smile. Soldiers were lined up either side of him, wielding silver weapons. Gregory knew how deadly they could be. The wolves would have to count on the humans for protection.

"Well you see my Queen," derision dripped from his words, "I think that to slay a beast, you need a beast, so I'd like to introduce you to my abomination." He gestured to some guards behind him who slowly opened the cage door. From the shadows a hulking beast emerged, bigger than any that Gregory had seen before. Its arms were as thick as trees and its claws were like talons. Its body was swollen with muscle and it seemed to bristle with anger, but as it came into view there was something else about the beast...something familiar.

"No..." Gregory whispered.

"What have you done? What have you done to my father?" Leah said in a voice as cold as winter's heart.

King Stewart laughed, throwing his head back. The abomination was in chains. It roared and spittle flew from its mouth. Its eyes were wild and the chains rattled loudly.

"I poisoned his blood. It's quite interesting the things you can do to a person with the right material. Silvain has always been rich in silver, but these mountains have provided other things as well. Now, you can know what it is to be slaughtered by your father, by your king," he spat and guided his horse away. The guards freed the abomination from the chains and all hell broke loose.

The abomination roared and beat its mighty fists on the ground as it charged forward. The Silvainian herded it by firing arrows, directing it at the Lycanthian forces. Its hide was so thick no weapon could penetrate it. Meanwhile, other silver arrows flew through the air and fell like hail among the wolves. Gregory twisted as he saw wolves fall. He looked to Leah. Should they retreat? Leah's face was twisted in rage. She flung her arm forward. Gregory followed the order. The only thing to do was attack.

The humans rushed forward, trying to head off the Silvainian army and get their attention to stop them from firing at the wolves. Ferdinand led the charge. Gregory was pleased that Leah was holding back. He knew she would have been itching to join the fight. If she had still been a wolf there was nothing that could have stopped her, so he fought twice as fiercely for her. He howled and led his wolves forward.

Some split off and attacked the Silvainian guards, getting revenge for all their fallen friends. They mauled and clawed, and the air was filled with screams and the ground was soaked in the dark shadows of blood.

But Gregory and the other wolves headed straight to the abomination, to the thing that had once been their king. It flung its arms out. Gregory watched a wolf run directly at it. The beast caught it and lifted it over its head, ripping it in two. Gregory ran over trembling ground and lunged at the beast, trying to find a weak spot. He nipped at heels, slashed through thighs. Fists almost beat him, but Gregory was just quick enough to escape. Not all were so lucky. He heard the sickening crunch of bone as the abomination's fists crashed into the side of a wolf's head. The wolf whimpered, and then it was silent.

A few wolves attacked in tandem and leapt upon the abomination. He roared and reached behind him, trying to fling them from his back. The wolves tore away flesh, sinking their teeth deep into the abomination's skin. Black blood trickled from the wounds, but still the abomination fought. It didn't seem like anything could stop him, and Gregory got the sense that Stewart would guide the abomination towards Lycanthia and use it to destroy the entire kingdom. Gregory was a blur as he whipped around. He howled loudly, trying to get the beast's attention to save another. Gregory dodged one set of slashing claws. He jumped up and scratched at the abomination's abdomen, but then the other arm came around and he was shot back. He whimpered in pain as he slumped to the ground, and as he looked up into the abomination's eyes he wondered if there was any part of the king left inside.

He rolled out of the way as the beast stomped near him, trying to crush him.

In the distance he saw the human armies engaging. The Lycanthians fought with pride and righteous fury. Without the advantage of a trap and the terrain of Maugrim's Pass, the Silvainian army seemed far less intimidating. Casper and Ferdinand were dueling, and Gregory was delighted to see Ferdinand spike Casper on his lance, punching through Casper's chest. He slumped and fell from his horse as Ferdinand wheeled away in triumph, leading his men on to victory.

Gregory only wished his side of the battle was going as well. Wolves were slumped around him, some dead, others merely wounded. On shaking limbs, he pulled himself up. The abomination was raging. The taste of blood filled Gregory's mouth. Every breath was a labor and he had no idea how he was going to win. When he let out a rallying howl, the sound was reedy and mewling. He walked forward, step by step, ready to fight to the last. He couldn't let this thing get to Leah or to Lycanthia. But how was he going to stop it? He watched as the abomination fended off another attack from a trio of wolves effortlessly. Gregory looked down at his paw and flexed his claws. Never before had he felt so powerless as a wolf and then it occurred to him. Perhaps he couldn't win as a wolf.

He roared in pain as he shifted. The agony almost made him faint. He looked around and saw a silver arrow that had been embedded in the ground. He picked it up, took aim, and flung it at the abomination. It thudded into the beast's back and he howled in pain. It was still vulnerable to silver. Gregory cried out to anyone who was listening as he whirled around and picked up as many arrows as he could, flinging them towards the abomination, but of course it only meant that Gregory had caught its attention. It came bearing down on him as Gregory backed away, fearing that this was the end of his life, that he would never see his son grow up. He raised his hands and closed his eyes, ready to embrace death.

"FATHER STOP!" Leah cried out. Gregory looked up and saw the Queen standing in the middle of the battlefield. She held a silver spear and glared at the abomination. The beast turned.

"If there's any part of you in there, please, stop this father. Fight back. I don't care if this king has poisoned you. You can fight back. You are not this monster. You are a noble king. You are my father and I…I need you," her voice cracked on the last word. The beast tilted its head and then Gregory saw something remarkable. It stopped and sank to its knees. It looked at its hands and the bloodshed it had caused, and then it howled to the moon.

***

Ferdinand brought Stewart to Leah's side.

"It doesn't matter what you do. I've won. Look at all the destruction, the death, and no wolf shall ever sit on the throne of Lycanthia again," the cruel king spat.

Leah took her spear and snarled at him. "You're wrong. I'm still a wolf. I always will be," she said, and thrust the spear in the king's neck. He fell back clutching his wound, and died in a pool of blood. Leah turned to her father and watched as he shifted back into a man.

"The dreams I...I thought the dreams were coming true," he gasped. He sank to a frail man. The wounds and the ordeal were too much for him to bear. The silver arrows punctured his skin and blood streaked out. Leah caught him. She told him that she was married and that he had saved her life. She promised him that Lycanthia would be safe. He clasped her hand, and then he died.

***

They carried King Boris' body back to Lycanthia so it could be given a proper burial. Tristan was aghast at what had happened, but said he was glad that Boris was at peace now.

"He suffered from terrible dreams. I imagine he thought they had all been leading to this moment, but he never would have harmed anyone he cared about. Never." Leah clung to Ferdinand and wept.

Gregory nursed his wounds and hugged Jack tightly. The threat against Lycanthia was over. The wolves had saved the day, and it was now a secret no longer. Everyone knew that wolves prowled Lycanthia, and the enemies were wise to stay away. When Gregory looked at his son he saw a bright future ahead, and he knew that everything was going to be okay. He kissed Jack and let love enter his heart before he rested from the ordeal. It was all going to be safe now that the threat from Silvain had been dealt with. Gregory gathered all the wolves in a Gathering, but this time he invited all the humans who mattered to them as well, and they remembered everything that had happened to them. All the names through history were repeated, and they vowed that no longer would wolves have to hide.

Michael was celebrated as the first child born to a new era.

Thus, ends the legend of Lycanthia.